SUPREMACIST

a novel by

DAVID SHAPIRO

New York City

TYRANT BOOKS
426 West 46th Street, Apt. D, New York City 10036

Printed in the People's Republic of China
First edition, 2016

Designed by Ryan P Kirby
www.nytyrant.com

SUPREMACIST

Dedicated to those who posted, and to those
who moderated, as I lurked

CHAPTER I

I slept on one of the couches in Camilla's living room, using my packed duffel bag as a pillow and my jacket as a blanket. The call from the car service woke me up. The driver said he was downstairs and I said, "We're on our way down now."

I sat up on the couch and put my sneakers on and walked into Camilla's room, where she was sleeping. It was 4:15 a.m. I rubbed my eyes. I lifted the blanket and tickled her feet to wake her up. She grumbled and turned over.

I said, "We have to get up, the car service is here."

She kicked her feet up to get my hands away and tucked them back under the blanket. She grumbled again.

She said, "You were so drunk last night. Just, like, charmless. You came over and passed out. And tried to tell me about Supreme but couldn't remember what you wanted to say. Do you remember that?"

I said, "Not vividly."

She said, "I thought we were going to go over our plans again?"

I said, "It's too late to change anything anyway."

She said, "Don't get that drunk on the trip please."

I said, "I'll try not to. But can we leave now? The car service is here. We're going to miss the plane. I've never missed a plane before. I don't know what happens."

Camilla was unmoved. She groaned.

I pleaded, "They're going to put us in a special lounge for people who've missed their flights, like detention in school. And make us pay like $500 to get onto another flight and then make us sit in the row in front of the bathroom."

Camilla said, "You don't know what you're talking about."

I said, "I know. That's why I started by saying, essentially, that I didn't know what I was talking about."

CHAPTER II

I felt like Camilla's little brother even though we were both 26. She was about the same height as me but seemed taller because she was a woman. She dated people who were either older or the same age as us but already had careers.

She got dressed while I went into the bathroom, took a milligram of Ativan with two shots of vodka, blew my nose, took another shot, stuffed the bottle down into the bottom of the garbage can and covered it in toilet paper so she wouldn't see it, and used her mouthwash for my breath.

I looked at my face in the mirror. Covered in a thin film of grease. I walked back into her room and sat down next to her on her bed while she was putting her shoes on.

I said, "I'm covered in a thin film of grease. I should have gotten up earlier to shower. I'm going to feel disgusting all day."

She said, "You reek. Did you literally *just* drink or is it from last night? Are you drunk right now?"

I was only buzzed. It was still setting in.

I said, "I'm not drunk. Can we go? The car service guy is going to leave."

My phone rang again. It was the driver. He was getting impatient with me.

CHAPTER III

The driver let us smoke cigarettes in the back of the car with the windows open. We drove east on the BQE. We sat in silence and smoked. I felt nauseous.

Camilla scrolled through Instagram on her phone.

I said, "I don't have anything to think about. Can we talk?"

Camilla said, "Why don't you look at your phone?"

I said, "I get carsick."

Camilla looked back at her phone.

She said, "I'm busy."

I took mine out and texted her, "🐀 🕊". She smiled.

We got onto the plane and it took off. I laid my head on Camilla's shoulder. It was bony. She slept with her mouth open and her pink beanie pulled down over her eyes. The light coming through the airplane window next to her put her face into relief. I could see each blonde hair individually when I focused. I tried to fall asleep.

In college, Camilla told my roommate that she wasn't sexually interested in me, so I never tried to sleep with her. If our friends found out that I'd failed, it would be too embarrassing. I would still have had to see her everywhere. And if she didn't want to see me any more, my friends would take her side and stop seeing me. She's more likable. I don't know if I'm very likable, but people need people to be with, to text, to be meat in the room at their birthday parties, and there are some people even less likable than me. So we became friends.

Camilla stayed in a house on Martha's Vineyard every summer and she invited her friends to stay at the house some weekends. Some years, I brought my girlfriends.

One year, when I had no girlfriend, I tried to sleep with one of Camilla's friends. Rachel. We drove to Martha's Vineyard together in my mom's car and I sang along, quietly, to show her that I knew the words, to some of the songs she played through the car stereo off her iPhone. She was surprised that I knew the words. "King of the Road" by Roger Miller. We were together in the car for a long time and it felt like something was going to happen, but when we got to the house and got out of the car, there were other people who she could talk to besides me. And I'd run out of conversation. And she didn't seem as interested in talking to me. I understood that.

Camilla had a lot of money. She never talked about it. In college, I kept asking her how much she was worth. But she wouldn't tell me. To get her to open up, I volunteered some financial information of my own. I told her, "I inherited $50,000 from my grandma when she died."

Camilla laughed. She still wouldn't tell me.

I proposed marriage. I said, "Will you marry me? I would be marrying you for money, but I would make it worthwhile for you. I would do chores and stuff. And it could be an open marriage. A sexless open marriage. Is there a word for that? A marriage so open that the people don't even have sex with each other, only other people?"

She said, "I bet there's a term of art for it, like on online forums for people in sexless open marriages. Or Craigslist. Like, they would identify themselves in their bios as '33/F/NY/SOM.'"

I asked again, "Will you marry me?" But she said no.

After college, while I worked as a paralegal at my uncle's law firm and tried to become a professional writer, she moved to California, North Carolina, and then a farm in Nicaragua.

It didn't work out for me. I wrote a few small newspaper stories and stories on magazines' websites.

And then, on Facebook, I saw that she was living in Brooklyn again. I guess it didn't work out for her either, whatever she was doing.

I called her, we talked for five minutes, and then I asked her to come with me on a trip around the world to go to every Supreme store.

I said, "Los Angeles, six in Japan, and London. And New York."

She said, "Yeah, sure, why not?"

I was surprised. I said, "Wait, are you sure? You don't, like, have to think about it?"

She said, "Nope. I'm not doing anything in January. What's Supreme?"

I said, "It's a men's skate brand. Or, like, a skateboard-inspired clothing brand. The logo is like the red rectangle with the word 'Supreme' in white lettering, bolded and italicized, inside the rectangle. You know what I'm talking about?"

She said, "I think so? I think I can picture it. This guy I dated in California wore it. But why do you have to go to the stores? Can you not just order the stuff online?"

I said, "I do order it online, but I'm not going to the stores to buy stuff. I'm going to them just to go to them. They're like museums for me."

She said, "But they're… Skate shops?"

I said, "It's complicated. I don't know if I can explain now."

She said, "Is it a cool brand?"

I said, "I think there is no such thing as a cool brand. I mean, there is no way that it could be cool to buy a piece of clothing with a brand on it and wear it as a declaration of your identity. But if, in your conception, there could be such a thing as a cool brand, yeah, I think Supreme would be a cool brand. I think one of the only cool brands, because only maybe five or six other brands are not corny, and Supreme, to me, is not corny. But it's more than being not corny. I guess, like, I would say Supreme is a long-term conceptual art project about capitalism, consumerism, property-as-theft, corporate destruction, ideas like that. I don't understand it fully. But it operates, technically, as a skateboarding-inspired men's clothing brand."

I thought about that for a second. I said, "Consumerism is such a corny word."

And then I said, "Actually, I take that whole thing back. Everything I said was corny and didactic. I don't know exactly what Supreme is. I guess that's why I want to go on this trip. I'm trying to figure it out. But, ostensibly, it's a skateboarding-inspired men's clothing brand."

CHAPTER IV

I fell asleep on the plane for what felt like a few hours but turned out to be only twenty minutes. I hadn't eaten in a long time, since lunch the day before, which I guess was about eighteen hours. I was sweating and felt panicky. The passenger sitting next to me had a bag of peanut butter M&M's tucked into the seatback in front of him.

I ate them. I got a piece of gum from Camilla's bag and chewed it so my breath wasn't chocolatey. I felt better. I fell asleep on Camilla's shoulder. When the plane landed, the guy whose M&M's I ate gave me a puzzled look. I looked at him like, "Why are you looking at me like that?"

CHAPTER V

We rented a car and Camilla drove us to her friend Victoria's house in Beverly Hills. I wanted to go straight to Supreme but Camilla wanted to put her bags down and see her friend.

She said, "It's impolite if we just arrive and ignore our host until it's convenient for us. And *you* should take a shower."

I went to college with Camilla and Victoria. Victoria majored in Egyptology, her father produced *The Usual Suspects*, and her mother used to be a model. She had red hair and a perfectly shaped behind. I remembered it from college. It would be profane to call it an ass.

We put our bags down in the spare bedroom and I stood with Victoria in her kitchen. Victoria wore leggings and I thought about squeezing her behind with my pointer and middle finger to test its firmness. Partially out of curiosity, like squeezing a body builder's bicep.

I looked away from Victoria because she made me feel lecherous. I felt like I should be a good houseguest.

I went to the bathroom, took an Ativan, and came back into the kitchen. Camilla and Victoria talked about where we should go to dinner. They named some restaurants while I furtively Googled the restaurant menus on my phone to look at the prices.

I had to ask my parents to take $8,000 out of the bank

account with the money my grandma left me when she died to go on this trip. I already paid like $3,000 for the plane tickets. I had $2,040 in cash in my wallet, which made me feel successful, walking around with so much money in my wallet, even though I didn't earn it.

Camilla asked, "Why are you glued to your phone right now?"

I said, "I'm busy." There were always pressing affairs to attend to on the cell phone for a busy guy like me. Always a lot of people getting in touch with me. I texted my mom, "Arrived safely".

I asked Victoria if she had anything to drink and she said there was a liquor cabinet in the living room.

Camilla looked at me like, "Remember what we talked about?"

I found some Kirkland Signature brand vodka. I said, loud enough so they could hear me in the kitchen, "I didn't know Kirkland Signature made vodka."

Victoria asked, loud enough so I could hear her in the living room, "Do you want a mixer? Or ice?"

I said, "I'm good. Thank you though."

I poured some vodka from the bottle into my mouth without touching the rim to my mouth, standing in the middle of the living room.

Victoria walked into the living room and looked at me pouring another mouthful of vodka in, with my legs apart for balance.

She said, "Do you want a *glass?*"

I said, nonchalantly, "No, it's okay, that's just another thing to wash." I thought, "Literally, I must be the most considerate houseguest on earth."

Camilla laughed nervously in the kitchen. Victoria walked back into the kitchen. I could hear Camilla whisper, "It's fine. He's weird."

Victoria whispered something I couldn't make out with

certainty, but it sounded like she said, "Clearly."

I walked back into the kitchen. When they mentioned a restaurant that they both seemed open to eating at, I looked up the menu on my phone, "to see if there's anything I'm in the mood to eat there."

The prices were reasonable.

I said, "This place looks awesome, we should definitely eat here. Can we eat here? I'm really in the mood for Italian food."

They both agreed. I applied my force of will and it worked. At the bottom of the menu, past the dinner section, there was a section for coffee and dessert.

I said, "Why is there an option for coffee after dinner?"

Camilla said, "They have that at most restaurants."

I said, "No, I mean, like, why is it a convention? It seems like it would just keep you awake too late."

Victoria shrugged.

I said, "I don't understand. It seems like after dinner would be the worst time to have coffee. Not to do George Costanza, like in the episode where a woman asks him to come up for coffee after dinner and he refuses, not realizing that she's asking him to have sex, but this isn't a sex thing – the restaurant itself is proposing it. *And,* if you have coffee at the restaurant, it eliminates one of the possible ostensible non-sexual auspices for one adult to invite another up to their apartment after dinner. I've seen adults actually do it. My parents have coffee after dinner sometimes."

Camilla said, "Why don't you ask your parents why they do it?"

Victoria said, "Maybe it aids digestion?"

I said, "Does 'aids digestion' mean it's therapeutic for your digestive system as a whole? Like, helps you get the nutrients out of what you just ate? Or is it a euphemism for 'makes you crap'? Or is it a longer-term thing than just one crap, like 'moves all the food through your digestive system faster'?"

Victoria said, in a tone I couldn't decipher, "It's a treat to hear you dissect language."

I didn't know how to respond because I couldn't tell if she was making fun of me.

Camilla joked, "You're a smart guy."

They both laughed. She was making fun of me. Maybe it was a stupid thing to say.

I leaned up against the kitchen island and tried to laugh, but I couldn't. I understood why they were laughing but it would feel false to laugh at myself. I tried to smile but my face just looked contorted, like a grimace.

I wished there was a pill I could take that would allow me to put my face into a natural smiling position so I could look normal. I guess everyone wishes for this. I should have become a pharmaceutical scientist to invent the pills I needed.

CHAPTER VI

We drove to the restaurant. I sat in the back seat like a little kid. Victoria and Camilla talked about what their mutual friends from college are doing now. Mostly working at *Buzz-Feed* and similar. I wished I worked at *BuzzFeed*.

Victoria said to me, "So you're into fashion now?"

I said, "I'm not, really. Supreme is the only thing in fashion that I like."

Victoria asked, "Do you skate?"

I said, "I can't. I can't balance on the skateboard. I tried a few times in high school and college, but I always fall off. The last time I tried, I fell off, hit the back of my head on the ground, and my glasses flew off and one of the lenses broke. It was a very Milhouse Van Houten thing to happen."

Victoria rolled her eyes. I could see it in the rear-view mirror.

I continued, "I'm afraid of heights, and, I don't know why, I get the same feeling when I stand on a skateboard as I do when I look down from a height. The ground seems far away, even if it's just a few inches. I tried to use a skateboard with small wheels to be closer to the ground, but it didn't work. Maybe I have a fear of being off the ground more than a fear of heights? But there's a popular conception of 'fear of heights,' but not one for 'fear of being off the ground,' so 'fear of being off the ground' sounds stupid, so I don't say it."

CHAPTER VII

We ate dinner at the restaurant. I got a gluten-free personal pizza. Victoria talked about her little brother.

She said, "He's getting really involved with church. It's freaky."

I asked, "How old is he?"

She said, "Sixteen."

I said, "Can I meet him?" I don't know why.

Victoria said, "No," and they both laughed.

Camilla said, "Are your parents religious?"

Victoria said, "Not at all. That's what's so weird about it. He's more religious than my parents. He thinks that because they don't go to church, they're… Probably going to go to hell. And that's compounded by the fact that they didn't take us to church either. He thinks they may have incidentally damned him too."

Camilla said, "That makes sense internally."

I asked, "Is he normal?"

Victoria said, "I think he's a little autistic. He knows the brand, model, and year of every single car on the road. But he goes to school normally."

I said, "What about trucks?"

Victoria said, "Oh yeah, every truck. And every city bus. And when he was little, he used to make my Dad take him to Union Station to look at the trains."

I said, "Well, at least he won't get any girls pregnant."

I waited for them to laugh at my joke, but nothing. Maybe they'd been pregnant.

I thought for a second. I said, "It's not Scientology, right? I know Scientology is big in Los Angeles." Victoria shook her head.

Camilla said, "Scientology gets a raw deal."

I said, "Because it's horrible."

Camilla said, "Yeah, but, like, who gives a shit? *Veal* is horrible. America is obsessed with Scientology being horrible only because celebrities do it. Do you know how many Scientologists there are in America?"

I said, "A couple million I think."

Camilla said, "*Maybe* 50,000."

I said, "No way."

Victoria Googled it.

Victoria said, "She's right. *The Village Voice* says there are probably only 25,000 in America. They say there are more Rastafarians than Scientologists in America."

I said, "I stand corrected," and looked away.

I said, "Does anyone want the rest of my pizza?"

I hated losing data-based arguments. It undermined all of the rest of my arguments. My assertions wouldn't be taken seriously at least for the rest of that dinner.

CHAPTER VIII

We were still eating. Victoria asked me, "If you don't like fashion and you can't skateboard, can you tell me why you're going on a trip to every Supreme store in the world?"

I said, "Are you familiar with the brand?"

Victoria said, "A guy I used to date wore it."

Camilla said, "Me too."

I said to Victoria, "Was he a cool guy?"

Victoria said, "I mean, sure. Who cares? Why are you going on this trip?"

I said, "It's hard to explain. I feel a strong connection to Supreme. Stronger than to anything else except maybe my parents. It's, like, the only thing I still believe in."

Victoria joked, "Do you have a sister who's worried about you because you think she and your parents don't wear enough Supreme?"

I said, "I'm an only child. Also, I have to think about this question more for a second. I guess part of the reason I want to go to every Supreme store is to come up with a satisfactory answer to the question, 'Why are you going to every Supreme store?'"

Camilla asked, "People ask you that?"

I said, "Sometimes, yes, when they notice that everything I wear says Supreme on it. Except the socks and underwear. They don't make those. And then when they point it out, I tell them I'm going on a trip to every Supreme store in the world. At least for the last few months. And then they ask why."

Victoria said, "It sounds like you could have just skipped going on the trip by not saying you were going on the trip in the first place."

I said, "But I want to go on the trip. I love to talk about Supreme. Just to talk and think about it makes me feel better."

Victoria looked at Camilla.

Victoria asked Camilla, "Why are you going on this trip?"

Camilla said, "I wasn't doing anything in January."

Victoria said, "That's it?"

Camilla said, "And I wanted to make Ian," a guy she was seeing, "jealous that I was going on a trip with another guy."

Victoria asked, "Did you tell him it was romantic?"

Camilla said, "He asked me if it was and I told him, 'Yes and no.'"

Camilla looked at me for a second. She looked self-conscious, like she was retroactively asking my permission to describe this trip as romantic. She'd never given me that look before.

I knew the guy. He invited me to his parties sometimes, and when he didn't, I tagged along with people he had invited. And he wasn't even standoffish about it when I showed up uninvited, even though he purposely didn't invite me. I knew he took me off the email invite list. And I think he knew I knew. But I still didn't want him to think I was secretly sleeping with her.

Victoria asked me, "Why did you want to bring her?"

I said, "I've never been out of New York State for longer than ten consecutive days and –"

Camilla looked at me blankly. She said, "You're joking."

I shook my head.

I said, "Have to keep Gotham safe." That was what I said when people found out I wasn't well-traveled.

Victoria said, "What was the ten days?"

I said, "A road trip to Florida in college."

Camilla said, "Didn't you go to sleep away camp?"

I said, "Yes, but that was in upstate New York."

Victoria said, "Have you been outside the country?"

I said, "Just Canada. On a three-day rafting trip to Montreal with my bunk at sleep away camp."

I picked up my pizza and chewed another bite.

With my mouth open and full of food, I said, "I know I carry myself with a worldly air, but I am, in fact, a provincial ignoramus."

Victoria laughed. Finally, a joke that worked. I swallowed the pizza and then took a sip of water and swished it around my mouth to dislodge any crap that may have been between my teeth.

I said, "I pictured myself on the other side of the Earth, like five thousand miles away from everyone I know, in a country where I don't speak the language and not many people speak English, nauseous from being hung over and smoking too much, and very lonely, and… I think I could try to kill myself or something."

Neither of them said anything for a second.

Victoria said, "Can I ask an indelicate question? It's relevant to your traveling partner."

I asked, "Can I guess what the question is?"

She asked, "Have you tried to kill yourself before?"

I said, "No, but the thought has crossed my mind obviously."

Camilla said, "Seriously?"

I said, "Yeah, but, I mean, not *seriously*. Doesn't everyone? Right? And you wonder who's going to come to your funeral? Especially in Japan, where, like, you know... Suicide. It's, like, the thing there. As I understand it. With swords, right? But, again, I am ignorant."

Victoria shrugged.

I continued, "Everything I know about actually being in Japan comes from *Lost in Translation*, i.e., it's isolating for

Americans. I also know they hate the Chinese and the toilets are sophisticated. And I love the flag, the red circle with the white background. That's why the Japanese love Supreme so much. Because they know great design."

Camilla said, "You're bringing me on this trip to prevent you from killing yourself?"

I said, "Is that, like, not a legitimate reason? I think there literally is no more legitimate reason for going on a trip around the world than to prevent someone from killing themselves. I get to go on a personal journey to understand Supreme and you get to go on both a pleasure trip around the world and a humanitarian mission."

Camilla looked at me like she couldn't tell if I was being serious.

I said, "Not only from killing myself, but also for companionship, and, like, the general comforting presence of a woman. Any woman who is more mentally stable than me would work. And you happened to be free at a time that coincided with my winter break from school."

Victoria said, "You're still in school?"

I said, "I'm in grad school. I'm becoming an actuary."

She gave me a puzzled look.

I said, "An actuary analyzes data to calculate things like insurance risks and, like, the values of intangible things."

Victoria said, *"Why?"*

I said, "It's a stable career. And it's interesting. Like, if someone chopped my leg off, and they caught the person, how much would the person have to pay me? Like, what's the dollar value of my leg?"

Victoria said, "Do you actually know what it is?"

I said, "Maybe, like, $1,250,000? $1,750,000? Something like that."

Victoria said, "Cool."

I said, "Wanna hear something interesting and sort of related? I learned it in school."

Victoria shrugged.

I said, "In the Talmud, which is, like, the official Jewish interpretation of the Old Testament, they had to calculate the penalty for rape, and they divided the penalty for rape by whether the woman was married or unmarried – if you raped a married woman, you would get put to death. But if you raped an unmarried woman, you would either have to pay her family the amount it would cost you to support her financially for the rest of her life *or* she could decide if she wanted to marry you. And you couldn't refuse. You would *have* to marry her. And you could never divorce her. Because in ancient times, women weren't allowed to work, and by raping an un-married woman, it meant nobody else would marry her, and so you'd deprived her of her livelihood, i.e., being supported by a husband."

Neither of them said anything for a second.

I said, "Pretty actuarial."

Camilla looked at Victoria, who was looking at her plate.

I said, "Wanna hear another one?"

Neither of them said anything.

I said, "I mean another thing from the Talmud. I love the Talmud."

Victoria said, "I have to go to the bathroom." She got up and went to the bathroom.

I knew I'd said the wrong thing. Camilla looked mad. The muscles in her jaw moved like she was clenching her teeth.

She said, "Do you realize, when you talk, that whoever you're talking to may have been sexually assaulted?"

I felt embarrassed. I wanted to crawl under the table. I took an Ativan out of my pocket and put it under my tongue.

I said, "I feel bad. Should I apologize to her?"

Camilla said, "I don't know. If you want, I guess. But it would be awkward if you just did it right away. She wanted to get away from that conversation."

We sat in silence. Camilla took out her phone.

I said, "What about when she asked me if I'd ever tried to kill myself?"

Camilla said, "It's different. You brought that up. She didn't bring up having to choose to marry your rapist to feed yourself."

I said, "Well, you don't *have* to marry your rapist. That's the thing – you can get the money instead."

She looked at me blankly. Her mouth hung open a little.

I said, "Okay, let's talk about something else and then I'll see if I can weave an apology in discreetly later."

Camilla said, "Yeah, let's." She went back to her phone.

Victoria came back from the bathroom and I tried to make eye contact with her but I couldn't. Victoria and Camilla talked about Victoria's job. She hated her boss. I couldn't look at them.

CHAPTER IX

We drove home and I sat silently in the backseat.

Camilla half-turned around and said, "By the way, I am not going to comfort you. Now that you've said you brought me on this trip to comfort you, I'm specifically not. I'm going to go out of my way not to. If you look uncomfortable, I'm going to find out why and try to exacerbate it."

I thought of saying, "What if it's something like that I'm afraid of spiders? And you're also afraid of spiders. If we saw one, would you pick it up and put it in my face? Like, how far would you go?" But I didn't say anything.

Camilla continued, "And I hope you made me the beneficiary on your life insurance policy, so if you do kill yourself, I can at least recoup my expenses for this trip."

I said, "I don't think I have life insurance? Also, you are going to comfort me. You have no choice. Just, like, your presence. Also, that's not *the only* reason. I also like hanging out. With you."

Victoria looked at Camilla in the front seat.

We stopped at a gas station. Camilla went into the convenience store to buy beer.

I got out of the car and stood next to Victoria as she was getting her credit card out of her wallet.

I asked Victoria, "Can I pay for the gas?"

She said, "No, it's fine."

I said, "Could I at least pump it?"

She shrugged and put her credit card into the machine. I took the hose and put it into the car and squeezed.

Victoria said, "What's the deal?"

I said, "With what?"

Victoria said, "Like… Are you trying to sleep with her? Or date her? I don't understand why you're bringing her."

I said, "I already said why I was bringing her."

Victoria said, "If you're doing some weird thing where you're bringing her to Japan to get her to like you or sleep with you… It would just be really weird."

I said, "Hey, she volunteered."

Neither of us said anything.

I said, "And I'm really sorry about the Talmud thing. I know it's horrific. I guess I just felt some distance from it because, like… I don't know. You know? I don't know. I'm sorry. But I didn't mean to make light of it. I just thought it was interesting."

Victoria said, "It's fine."

I said, "Also, before I forget, thanks for letting us stay with you."

She shrugged and nodded.

We stood there for a second.

I said, "I love the smell of gasoline at gas stations. That's common, right?"

Victoria said, "She told me you asked her to marry you."

I said, "It was in college! And I was joking. And that was like eight years ago. Our relationship has always been friends without benefits. She's hung out with like two or three of my girlfriends."

The pump clicked because the tank was full. I squeezed it a few more times to top it off. I pulled it out slowly, squeezing as I pulled so the sensor wouldn't detect the tank was full. I peered into the tank as I pulled and squeezed to make sure it wasn't about to overflow. As a houseguest, I tried to go above and beyond.

CHAPTER X

We drove towards Victoria's house again in silence. On the freeway, I looked out the window at all of the lanes, probably like six lanes. The only thing I'd noticed about Los Angeles so far was that more of the billboards there seemed to be for movies and TV shows than the billboards in New York.

Victoria said to me, "Have you thought of the rest of your answer to why you're doing this? I think it started with, 'Supreme means more to me than my own life.'" Camilla laughed.

I thought it would be more comfortable to have a conversation than to continue to sit in silence.

I said, "Are you sure you actually want to hear my whole thing? It's long. And, like, I don't know if it's interesting to anyone else besides me. You know?"

Camilla said, "We'll let you know as soon as it isn't."

I said, "Well, first, New York. That's the first thing. It's the only place I've ever lived. I couldn't imagine living anywhere else. As I said, I've never been out of the state for longer than ten days. I've been to San Francisco and LA and those are nice for other people, but, like, New York is my place. I know, me and however many million other people, but still, it's my place. I love it."

Camilla said, "Maybe because you haven't really been anywhere else."

I said, "Maybe. Or maybe because everywhere else is lame

for some reason or another. But anyway, so Supreme started in New York in 1994, a few days after Giuliani became mayor, which was January 1, 1994. Supreme opened a few days later on Lafayette Street. The rest of the street was basically desolate, like all of downtown. Air conditioner factories and stuff. My mom told me about seeing open drug deals and prostitution all over downtown. She lived uptown and she was afraid to go downtown. And it was the year *Illmatic* and *Ready to Die* came out. *Enter the 36 Chambers* came out the year before. It was a special time to be alive. In New York."

I continued, "And then, in the twenty-one years after Supreme opened, everything around it changed. David Bowie and Iman, the supermodel, live across the street from Supreme now. There's a coffee shop next door that sells cups of coffee for like $5. When we came to college in New York in 2006, it was hard to imagine that New York had been so shitty so recently. I feel like it's even changed in the eight years since we've lived there."

I leaned towards Camilla's seat and said, "Did you see they just knocked down the Salvation Army shelter on Bowery and 3rd?" We both lived in a dorm a block away from that shelter.

Camilla said, "I had no idea you were so 'I miss the old New York.' That's super corny. False nostalgia. You would never have lived in the old New York, and if you did, you would have lived uptown and voted for Giuliani."

I said, "I'm not so 'I miss the old New York.' I know I'm a beneficiary of New York being sanitized. I like being able to walk home alone at night without worrying about getting mugged. I wouldn't trade back. But there's definitely something different. Like, something lost."

Camilla said, "Have you seen *Rent?* You would love it."

I said, "Fuck you. Don't be mean."

I leaned towards Victoria's seat.

I said, "I can have false nostalgia, right? Why can't I? I'm allowed to think there's something romantic about open drug transactions on 14th Street, that I missed, and still prefer things the way they are now. It's not either/or. And I'm allowed to think there's something culturally upsetting about the 7/11 on Bowery and 4th Street, and the Bowery Hotel, and all the other corny garbage that's descended upon us. I have Tylenol in my bag that I bought at that 7/11. But I hate it for existing, and I hate it more knowing that it's there for people like me. I'm not unaware that I am the problem. But, like, where am I supposed to live?"

Camilla didn't say anything. Victoria said, "What does this have to do with Supreme?"

I said, "To me, Supreme is a living testament to the old New York. Supreme still does the same thing it always did even though everything around it changed. The clothes from 2000 look like the clothes from 1996, 2002, 2009, 2014. It's like 'The Brand That Time Forgot.' Or, like, you know, like the *Simon & Garfunkel* song 'The Only Living Boy in New York.' To me, it's one of the last remaining things that's still vibrant, and not just selling its own nostalgia, from a wilder and less expensive time. Supreme makes me think, like, of, like… I don't know, like, how my life could have been different in a wilder and less expensive time in New York. Like, maybe I wouldn't be going to actuary school."

Camilla said, "But you said you like actuary school."

I said, "I do like it. But I might have liked to do something different, like start a business, if it seemed like there was a reasonable possibility of doing that. Or be a reporter. The owner of Supreme opened the store with $12,000. And it's huge and in the middle of downtown Manhattan. That kind of thing would be impossible in Manhattan today. Or anywhere close, like in relevant Brooklyn. When Supreme opened, you could do what you wanted in New York with low overhead. Or smoke in a bar. I know that's true for any business that started before 1994 too, but, like, to me, Supreme is the last one. For Supreme, 1994 in New York was the end of history. It's stuck there. With the shittiness and the brusque-ness. Almost all of the clothes look like they were pulled off of a skater walking around downtown Manhattan in 1994. And the store employees are proudly assholes, like, I think, a lot of people were in New York before politer people, like us, colonized it. Like, 'Fuck You You Fuckin' Fuck'-type people."

I continued, "When I first walked past the store, in college, I was afraid to go inside. If they think you aren't the kind of person they want wearing Supreme, they look at you like you are dog shit. I love that. They used to go up behind customers, tap them on the shoulders, and whisper into their ears, 'No touching until you buy!' I don't think they still do that, but the way they look at you conveys the same message: 'Can I fuckin' help you?' How cool is that? They don't want your money if you're not worthy. It's like they believe in something more than money. Like terrorists. Or monks."

Camilla said, "I think they are interested in your money, but they realize that if you see undesirables wearing Supreme, they'll stop getting everyone's money after a while. A lot of brands operate like that. That's why, like, Chanel burns their unsold clothes instead of sending them to, like, Africa – they'd rather eat that money than have undesirables wearing it. This isn't special."

I said, "Well, okay, here's another thing – they sell the clothes for a lot less than they could."

Victoria said, "How much is, like, a t-shirt?"

I said, "Generally between $32 and $44."

Victoria said, "Not exactly T.J. Maxx."

I said, "I know, but people buy the clothes and then turn around and sell them on eBay for double or triple. Supreme could sell the clothes for a lot more. They know this. Does, like, Chanel sell handbags for a lot less than people are will-ing to pay?"

Victoria said, "Probably not…"

I said, "How much does a Chanel handbag cost?"

Victoria said, "Depends on the handbag. Maybe, like, $4,000?"

Camilla said, "You keep comparing it to Chanel, but it's just a skateboarding brand. It's not, like, couture."

I said, "It's *not* just a skateboarding brand. Damien Hirst and Jeff Koons design stuff for them and they just sell it for the same prices as the rest of the stuff even though it's worth, like, thousands of dollars. They sold Damien Hirst skateboard decks for like $50 that are on eBay now for like $10,000."

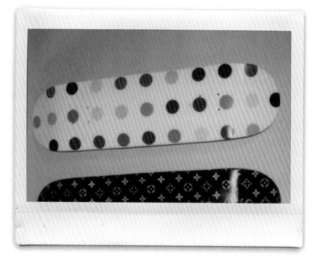

Camilla said, "Proenza Schouler designs stuff for Target."

I said, "That's a fashion designer?"

Camilla said, "Proenza Schouler is the name of a brand, not a person."

I said, "Who's a fashion designer who designs stuff for Target?"

Victoria said, "Prabal Gurung."

I said, "Well, Damien Hirst is not a fashion designer. Almost none of the people they collaborate with are fashion designers – they're artists. And Target probably paid Prabal Gurung a lot for that. She traded some of her credibility by selling cheap crap at Target for a lot of money. That's different from –"

Camilla said, "Prabal Gurung is not a woman."

I continued, "I don't think Damien Hirst, who sells skulls covered in diamonds for like $75,000,000, made stuff for Supreme so as to reap the profits of the sales of a few hundred t-shirts and skateboard decks."

Camilla said, "It's not so different if he does it for credibility. Because people like you think Supreme is authentic. People in creative industries seem to have knacks for turning authenticity into money, you know?"

I said, "He sells skulls for $75,000,000! He no longer has terrestrial concerns like money or credibility. When someone buys something you made for $75,000,000, *that* gives you credibility. I bet, if he wanted to, he could eat gold and find people to let him take gold-filled shits into their mouths. There would be a line outside of his house. It would be a rite of passage in the art world. And so –"

Camilla said, "I don't know why you think someone having money leads them to not care what other people think. The *only* thing rich people care about is what other people think of them."

I said, "I disagree."

Camilla said, "Can I offend you?"

I said, "It would be my pleasure to be offended by you right now."

Camilla said, "Only someone without money would say something like that."

I said, "Yeah, probably."

I sat there, not saying anything. What else would I say to a thing like that? And maybe she was right.

Victoria stopped the car at a light. She turned around and said to me, "But so he spends his days designing skateboards for Supreme instead of shitting into peoples' mouths?"

I said, "Yes! Yes. He designs skateboard decks for Supreme,

I guess, for the same reason I'm doing this trip – he believes in Supreme. It's *not* just a skateboarding brand. It's a long-term conceptual art project about consumerism and theft. And about New York. And all of the Giuliani and post-Giuliani things, like the 7/11 on Bowery. And, like, me. And corporate ownership. But what Supreme makes is more artful than writing, like, 'Die yuppie scum' on a t-shirt. The 'Fuck Giuliani' idea is pretty common, but, like, like a lot of common things, like bagels or something, it's hard to do it well. What Supreme does is –"

Camilla turned around and rolled her eyes.

She looked at Victoria and said to me, "Do people tell you you're a mansplainer?"

I said, "Victoria asked! She asked why I wanted to go on this trip and now I'm explaining! This isn't, like, an unsolicited explanation of something that I am oblivious to the fact that no one else is interested in because I am a man and I assume every woman is interested in every little thing I have to say."

I turned to Victoria. I said, "Right?" She shrugged.

I said to Camilla, "Are you being an asshole to me because of what I said at dinner?"

Camilla half-smiled. She said, "I'm just trying to push your buttons."

I said, "Just let me say my thing, okay?"

Camilla nodded.

I said, "The other thing is that I think Supreme runs the most visibly, to the public, illegal business I personally know of. Obviously there are huge companies that do illegal things, but they don't do them openly. Like, for example, oil companies buy stolen oil and then sell it at gas stations. I heard this on a podcast. The oil is stolen, in, like, Russia and Venezuela, and then put into tankers with non-stolen oil, and so the companies that turn the oil into gas for cars can't tell if the oil they're buying is stolen. Because it's all mixed together. But it's undeniable that, like, there's stolen oil in this car's gas tank.

This car we're riding in right now. And so –"

Victoria said, "What does this have to do with Supreme?"

I said, "The stolen oil market requires subterfuge. Shifty middlemen, falsified documents, bribing government officials. Supreme *openly* sells illegal –"

Victoria said, "Oil is like the second-most popular liquid on Earth after water. Supreme sells, like, some t-shirts. Supreme isn't that *visible*, as you said, I think. You said visible?"

I said, "In its sphere, Supreme is massive. For example, there's a men's fashion forum where people talk about different fashion brands. The thread about only the *current* Supreme season has more than ten million pageviews. More than forty thousand individual replies. Literally sixteen hundred *pages* of replies. Other big brands on the forum get maybe fifty thousand pageviews. And you can't use the thread to buy or sell stuff – there are separate threads for that. This thread is just peoples' *opinions* about Supreme. It's just people being, like, 'Yeah, this hoodie is sick. I'm gonna cop for sure.' It's, like, forty thousand farts in the wind about Supreme. And people smelling them ten million times."

I continued, "People are *obsessed* with Supreme. The only thing I can think to compare it to is Apple. Like, at the beginning of every season, people sleep outside the Supreme stores for days in order to get inside, just like the iPhone lines outside Apple Stores. The line outside Supreme is multiple blocks long. I wrote a newspaper story about it and I talked to the kid who was first in line who'd been waiting for six days. He does it every time a new season comes out. Sometimes, he doesn't even buy anything. He just goes in and looks around and is like, 'Eh, this season, I'm not really feeling it.' So Supreme is pretty visible, I think. In a certain world."

Camilla said, "How is what they do illegal?"

I said, "Some of what they make contains blatant trademark infringement. They just use other companies' logos. Like, in 2012, they made hats and hoodies that had a picture of

Eustace Tilley, *The New Yorker's* mascot, you know? With the pipe? That character with the butterfly and the bubble pipe? And the Supreme stuff just had Eustace Tilley and the word Supreme under it in *The New Yorker's* font. They didn't pay *The New Yorker* or ask to use it."

Victoria said, "How do you know they didn't get permission?"

I said, "I overheard people talking about it at a bar."

Victoria said, "What bar?"

I said, "Max Fish."

Camilla said, "You go to Max Fish?"

I said, "I *have* gone." I didn't really belong there. That's why she asked.

Camilla looked like she was listening more intently then.

I said, "Part of the fun of Supreme is getting the references, i.e., understanding what they're ripping off or referencing."

Victoria said, "Do you get the references?"

I said, "I get maybe 5% of them. But I think most of them are sports or fashion, and I don't really know from sports. But when a Supreme season comes out, it feels like all of the clothes are part of a puzzle.'"

I continued, "I read online this explanation of the phenomenon of Supreme as a hierarchy of people sneering at each other. Like, there are 13-year-olds from Westchester who make their parents take them to Supreme because they saw Drake wearing a Supreme jacket in a video. And there are 17-year-old skaters sneering at the 13-year-olds, who aren't worthy of Supreme because they're there with their parents. And they don't skate. And then there are 21-year-old fashion student skaters sneering at the 17-year-olds because the 17-year-olds don't get the fashion references, or even understand that there are references to get. And then, at the top of the hierarchy are the aggressively aloof store employees themselves, who are sneering at everyone except each other, because everyone else there is submitting to being silently tormented by their disapproving faces. And paying a lot of money to be part of some sort of joke they don't even realize is being made.

I continued, "Like, the ultimate joke of Supreme is on the customer. The receipts from the LA store say 'You are being lied to' on the bottom. Their logo is taken from Barbara Kruger, an anticonsumerist feminist artist, from a piece that says, 'I shop therefore I am.' They're making fun of the customer for being, like, a *customer*."

I said, "It's like how part of a piece of contemporary art is its own financial value? Like, a Picasso costs $15 million because Picasso advanced the rules of perspective in painting. And a Jeff Koons balloon dog sculpture costs $15 million because of its awareness that it costs $15 million. It has the audacity to cost $15 million. And when you buy a Jeff Koons balloon dog for $15 million, you're paying to be in on the joke, to take ownership of the joke, to demonstrate that *you* understand why a Jeff Koons balloon dog is worth $15 million. But even when you buy it, Jeff Koons is laughing at you. Because you can never really take ownership of his joke. Because you *are* the joke. You're the thing that makes a stupid balloon dog worth $15 million. Same thing with Supreme."

Camilla said, "What do you mean by 'the joke'?"

I said, "Like, the existence of money turns us all into idiots, into animals. I think that's the joke."

Camilla said, "What are you getting this from?"

I said, "Wikipedia, mostly. I started with the Damien Hirst shark in formaldehyde."

Victoria asked, "Where are you in the hierarchy of sneering?"

I said, "Low. I don't skate, I'm way too old to be wearing skateboarding stuff, and I can't even really affect aloofness. I guess the only thing that elevates me above the 13-year-olds is that I understand that there is some sort of joke to be in on. But maybe I'm below them, because I'm knowingly submitting to it. Like in Animal House, when Kevin Bacon is getting paddled on the ass? To be initiated into the fraternity? And he keeps saying, 'Thank you, sir! May I have another?!' That's how I feel every time I buy something. But, like, I'll never be in the fraternity – I'm a 26-year-old actuarial student. The people who work there look at me like dog shit. And I like it. I understand why they think I am dog shit. I am dog shit."

Victoria and Camilla laughed.

I continued, "Supreme has a set of mechanisms for dealing with the fact that some of the stuff they sell is illegal. First, companies whose logos they rip off might be flattered, and also wouldn't want to seem like bullies, like by suing them, because Supreme presents itself as a small New York operation, not a global brand."

I continued, "Second, they don't keep using the same trade-marked or copyrighted images over and over. Like, in 2013, they made a hat with Speedy Gonzales and the words 'ADIOS MUTHA' on it. But Warner Brothers owns Speedy Gonzales. Supreme only used Speedy Gonzales once, so it's less likely that Warner Brothers, or any individual trademark or copy-right owner, would find out. They don't fly that close to the sun, like by ripping off the same person over and over."

I continued, "Third, because they make small quantities of each item, it means that if the trademark owner ever *does* find out, the stuff is probably already sold out, so there's no sale left to cease-and-desist. You can't cease-and-desist something that's no longer happening. Like, they're not selling it any-more. They have *already* ceased and desisted from selling the thing. That means the only thing they can do is sue Supreme for damages."

I continued, "Fourth, if the trademark owner does find out, because they make small quantities of each item, it's probably not worth it to lawyer up over the proceeds of a few hats and t-shirts and stuff. Especially if it's not *that* clearly trademark infringement, like if the logo is changed slightly but still clearly a reference, because you might lose in the end anyway, and still look like an asshole for dragging Supreme, this small skateboarding company, into court."

I continued, "Fifth, if the trademark owner does happen to find out *and* cease-and-desist before the clothes sell out, sometimes, Supreme finds a way around it. Once, I went into Supreme and saw this hoodie with a Supreme logo that looked like the LA Kings hockey team logo on it. The tag said 'jeans.' When I bought it, I asked the guy behind the register why the tag said 'jeans,' and he said it was because the hockey team cease-and-desisted them. And so in their ledger, it looked like they'd sold a pair of jeans."

I continued, "And then, sixth, and this doesn't really count as an evasion mechanism, but sometimes, they do just get caught and eat it. Like, a long time ago, they made skateboard decks and t-shirts with the Louis Vuitton print on them. And Louis Vuitton cease-and-desisted them and made them pay for it."

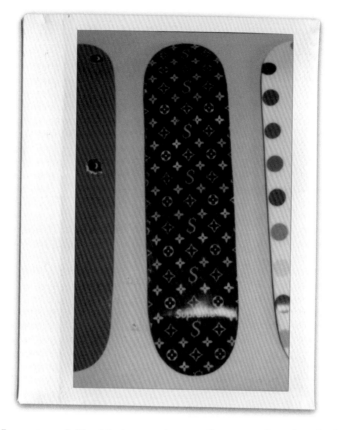

I continued, "Is this interesting at all to you? I can't tell if it's just me. I can keep going."

Camilla looked at Victoria and said, "We'll let you say one more thing."

I thought for a second. I said, "Okay. The best part about Supreme is that they have a sort of 'honor among thieves' attitude about what they do. Like, eBay is full of counterfeit Supreme stuff. And these aren't, like, carefully crafted fakes – they're crappy products that Supreme has never made with Supreme logos on them, selling for $19.99. But even though eBay makes it easy to report counterfeits, Supreme doesn't do anything to go after the counterfeiters."

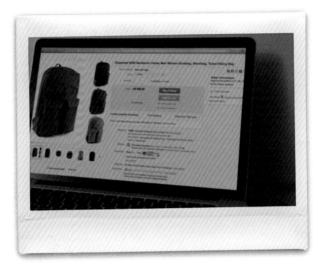

Victoria said, "How do you know?"

I said, "Before I went back to school, I was writing a story about Supreme suing someone for trademark infringement. I talked to the owner, who's a press-shy 49-year-old British guy. His name is James Jebbia. I emailed the general e-mail address on the Supreme website asking for a comment from the owner for my story. I thought Jebbia would never talk to me because there's a big *New York Times* story about Supreme and in it, the reporter writes about how he had to go back to Supreme three times and prove that he 'got' Supreme before Jebbia would talk to him. That he got that it wasn't just a skate brand like Etnies. That there was *something else* going on. Jebbia had only ever done a handful of interviews and they were always on his terms. So I thought he would never talk to me."

I continued, "But he called me immediately. He was furious. He didn't even introduce himself. He just started growling at me. I knew who it was. I felt so excited – it was like talking to the man behind the curtain in the *Wizard of Oz*. But at the same time, he was growling at me because he thought I was writing a story that suggested that Supreme was being hypocritical. He said they'd never sued someone for trademark infringement before, including the people who sell fake stuff on eBay. He said, 'I don't mind if someone else makes a buck off Supreme.' And then he was like, '*Why* are you writing this story?'"

Camilla said, "Who did they sue?"

I said, "A woman who was making a whole line of clothing that said 'Supreme Bitch' in the Supreme font and color scheme. It was popular. They were selling it at Urban Outfitters. And Supreme cease-and-desisted her. Originally, Supreme gave her permission to make the Supreme Bitch t-shirts. I think she was trying to make a point about Supreme being a boys' club, which it might be, I guess. They don't make women's clothing. But that's a different issue. But then, so anyway, after she got permission from Supreme to make the t-shirts, she made t-shirts, towels, hats, mousepads. A ton of different stuff. A whole line. She might have made, in total, more Supreme Bitch stuff than Supreme makes Supreme stuff.

I continued, "And so when Jebbia asked me why I was writing the story, I said, 'Well, I guess because of the irony of Supreme suing someone for infringing on your trademark when, like, obviously, like, you guys… Infringe on other peoples' trademarks.' I could barely get the words out of my mouth, accusing him of something."

Victoria said, "What did he say?"

I said, "He said it wasn't a fair or reasonable comparison. He said there's a difference between Supreme appropriating many companies' logos once and appropriating Supreme's logo hundreds of times, to build an entire clothing line. I guess he was trying to say that there's a difference between single acts of recontextualization and… Profiteering from the same act of recontextualization, over and over. A comment vs. a counterfeit. I thought he was pretty convincing. I guess, like, I think of what Supreme does as art. And I think of what

Supreme Bitch did as commerce."

Camilla said, "But that's just stealing a little bit from a lot of people versus stealing a lot from one person. Both are stealing. Both are commerce."

I said, "Are you playing devil's advocate or do you actually believe that they're the same?"

Camilla said, "I just don't see that much of a difference. And I think maybe you're predisposed to think what men do is art and what women do is commerce."

I said, "I don't think that at all! That's not a fair generalization! I am only talking about this one specific situation!" But maybe she was right.

I turned to Victoria.

I said to her, "Can you agree with me here? That my point could be the same absent gender? That it could be the same if the other brand was 'Supreme Motherfucker'?"

Victoria said, "I see what you're saying."

I said, "And the effect is different. Nobody is going to stop subscribing to *The New Yorker* if they see someone walking down the street in a hat with Eustace Tilley on it. And not that many people are seeing those hats anyway, because they don't make many. But people might stop buying Supreme stuff if they see Supreme Bitch and think it's corny. So all the damage that Supreme Bitch might cause would fall on Supreme's brand. And Supreme might not cause any damage to the brands they rip off. I mean, I guess, Louis Vuitton wouldn't want people to think they were making skateboard decks. So that's a little damage. But Supreme isn't a brand whose every product is a reference to another brand's signature product. Like, Supreme Bitch was like Yertle the Turtle, where one single turtle was on the bottom of a stack of turtles, feeling the weight of all the other turtles on top of him. And the companies Supreme rips off are like a pyramid of cheerleaders, where everyone feels a little bit of the weight distribution."

I turned to Camilla. I said, "Right? Can you see what I'm saying?"

Camilla said, "Yeah. Can we not talk about Supreme anymore?"

I said, "Okay, but I feel like I've overrepresented Supreme's trademark infringement. I think Supreme makes a lot of stuff that isn't remotely trademark infringement. I think, like, the vast majority of their stuff isn't. But it's cool that some stuff is."

Camilla said, "Or maybe you just don't get the references."

I said, "Maybe. But I know there's always *something* there. Like, to me, Supreme is about the end of an old New York, so I look for references like that. Like, one of Supreme's logos is from the credits to *Goodfellas.*

I continued, "But to someone else, who gets more of the fashion references, it might be about fashion. Or about corporate ownership of intellectual property being harmful to everyone. Or skateboarding. Supreme contains multitudes. And if it was clear exactly what they were, like if they made only shirts that said, 'Die yuppie scum,' it wouldn't be clever."

Camilla said, "And you wouldn't wear it."

I said, "Maybe I would. 'I am large, I contain multitudes.'"

Victoria said, "What's that from? 'I contain multitudes.'"

I said, "I remember it from high school. Like, Henry David Thoreau I think? The whole thing is like, 'Am I contradicting myself? That's not a problem, because I think a lot of stuff. I contain multitudes. I can think contradictory stuff.'"

We drove in silence for a little while.

I said, "I feel like, I guess, like, when you're a kid, and the adults are saying stuff and you don't understand it because they're talking about Gorbachev or something. And you don't know anything about Gorbachev. Or, like, a comedian is making jokes that go over your head and the adults are laughing. And then, when you get older, you watch the same comedian and realize what the adults were laughing at, but the jokes just aren't that funny. You get them, but they aren't that funny. I guess, I feel like I've gotten older, and started getting the jokes of society, and understanding things, and things, like, aren't that funny. Peoples' motivations are transparent and profane. God doesn't exist. People you thought were geniuses give interviews that reveal they're morons. That's the thing about adulthood, right? That everything you thought was magical starts to disappoint you? Because you start to 'get it,' but it's lame? And other people are lame? Like, every day you exist, you feel less wonder and mystery about the world? But for me, with Supreme, I still don't get the jokes. But I know they're there. And so I love it. I can't solve the puzzle."

Camilla said, "You've figured out everything else? Supreme is the only thing left that you don't understand?"

I thought for a while.

I said, "Supreme, women, how to conduct myself in public, and how to be a success in life."

I couldn't think of anything to say after that. We pulled into Victoria's driveway.

CHAPTER XI

I fell asleep in my clothes on the bed in the spare bedroom while Camilla and Victoria watched *Friends* and smoked marijuana. I hated *Friends*. I didn't want to tell Camilla. I hoped she secretly hated it too. Joey, the stupid guy with a big heart. I also hated smoking marijuana. It made me uncomfortable. I know saying "marijuana" sounds stupid, but all ways of referring to this drug eventually sound stupid. "Weed" and "joint" will sound like "grass" and "doobie".

Camilla came into the bedroom.

She woke me up and said, "How are we going to sleep? There's only one bed."

I said, "Do you want me to sleep on the floor? I can sleep on the floor?"

Camilla thought about this.

I half-joked, "We could both sleep in the bed if you promise not to try to touch my weenie while I'm sleeping."

She smiled and said, "Deal."

She went to the bathroom and came out wearing underwear and a t-shirt. Her blonde hair went half way down her back. I tried not to look at her body.

I said, "Do you want to watch *The Simpsons* on my iPad? I have the FXNOW app. You can watch any of *The Simpsons* episodes."

Camilla said, "I don't like *The Simpsons*."

I said, "Have you seen it? I mean, a lot of it. I think you'd need to see at least 60 or 70 episodes to judge it accurately."

She turned off the light and got into bed next to me.

I whispered, because the light was off and I used to have to whisper after lights-out at camp, "I'm sorry if I offended you with the Talmud thing. I didn't even consider that you would be offended, only that Victoria would, because you seemed mad that I'd offended her. That was nice of you, to be mad on behalf of your friend at the expense of yourself also."

She whispered, I guess because I whispered, "You didn't offend me. I know you didn't mean anything by it. But you don't understand that things that seem like issues of problem-solving rationality to you might not be the same for everyone."

I nodded. I whispered, "I know."

Light from a streetlight came in through the bedroom window above our heads. I felt shaky because I hadn't had a drink since the morning.

Camilla whispered, "If you'd been 26 in 1994, do you really think you would have opened a store? Or done something else creative?"

I whispered, "I would always have become an actuary, an accountant, a lawyer, a doctor, an engineer. One of those. My parents are lawyers. They wouldn't have been satisfied with me if I hadn't become a professional. But I *could* have. You know? And it's nice to fantasize about a New York where it would have been possible for me to do something besides be a professional and make enough money to have the kind of life I want."

Camilla said, "Or at least smoke in a bar." Maybe she was thinking the same thing.

I got up and went over to my luggage and got my vodka bottle out of it and filled my mouth and swallowed. It burned. I coughed.

Camilla said, "Why are you drinking now?"

I said, "I'll wake up in the middle of the night if I don't."

Camilla said, "Are you worried about that?"

I said, "What aspect?"

She said, "Being an alcoholic."

I said, "I'm on vacation – I can have a drink."

Camilla said, "What about when you're not on vacation?"

I said, "Later in life, I'll deal with it. I'll drink less. When I have a reason to."

She said, "Can I have some?"

I said, "Of course."

I came back to the bed and sat on the edge and handed her the bottle. She drank from it and grimaced. I drank more and we talked until I was drunk enough that I didn't feel any pressure to make conversation. And then I just sat there.

She said, "How do you feel?"

I said, "I'm in a fugue."

She laughed, and then lay down and went to sleep. I drank a little more.

I lay down and turned over onto my side and slept facing away from her.

CHAPTER XII

I woke up and vomited in the shower. I drove to Supreme with Camilla. We got there before it opened and waited outside. Supreme Los Angeles, the only other Supreme store I'd been to. I felt like I was home.

We browsed the clothing together. I touched every item. I knew the prices by heart. For some of the items, I knew the percentages of each material used to make them.

Camilla nodded and made utterances of approval as we went through the clothes. We stood in front of the Hi-Vis backpack with the reflective stripe. It might look just all right to you, but I loved it. It was just right.

She asked, "What's different here from the one in New York?"

I said, "It's exactly the same, and the same as the online store, except they sell a few t-shirts here from local designers that they don't sell at the New York store or online. But I'm not interested in those. Even the décor is the same – the white walls, the hardwood floors. Even the same shelving and the same bench. But there's no skateboarding bowl in New York. So I guess that's the part that's different."

I picked up the patent leather camp cap and examined it.

Camilla said, "Are you going to buy that?"

I whispered, so none of the employees could hear me, "Oh no, it's awful. Could you imagine a human being actually wearing this?"

She whispered, "You don't like all of this stuff?"

I shook my head.

She whispered, "I was pretending I liked all of it because I thought you did."

I whispered, "You don't have to do that. I know a lot of it is ugly."

Camilla looked around. There was an employee near us.

She whispered, "Can we go find a Diet Coke and come back? I want to talk about this outside."

I nodded. We walked outside and down the street towards Canter's.

I said, "I think most of what they make is embarrassing to be seen wearing. Not wearable in public. Like, for example, that jacket with the patch of Ronald Reagan's face on the sleeve.

I continued, "But I think they do it on purpose. Like, because they make small quantities of each item, if every piece of clothing they made was something that a lot of people liked, people would buy all of the clothing. Which seems like the object of a clothing store. But the store would be empty, and after a while, no one would come. Supreme wants to be a community center for skaters, so they want people to come, and to have some pretext for being in there – looking at the clothes. They come out with new clothes every week, every Thursday morning, so people have a reason to come back to the store every week. They could make greater quantities of each item, but part of the appeal of the brand is that every item is rare. So they can't make that much. And they have to make a bunch of unwearable clothing so there's something on the shelves."

Camilla asked, "Are you just making this up?"

I said, "One time, in college, I went into the New York store and looked at a jacket. I asked one of the employees if they had any left in my size. He said they didn't, and then he sort of laughed and said that they were shocked that *anyone* had bought this jacket, let alone that they'd sold out of it. He made it seem like the jacket was designed not to sell, like selling it contravened their intention for the product as something to draw people into the store to touch, talk about, and then come back the next week to do the same thing."

Camilla seemed like she was considering this.

We found a Diet Coke and came back to the store. Camilla sat on a bench in the middle of the store. I looked through the clothes again and again.

I couldn't stop buying Supreme stuff. I'd spent $15,000 on it. They were taking my money from me. Every item in the store that I might have wanted, I already had. Things I didn't even like. I didn't have any control over it.

She tapped me on the shoulder.

She said, "I'm bored."

I said, "I understand. You don't have to stay here."

She said, "How long are you going to stay here?"

I said, "Probably all day. Or, like, until they close. At 7:00."

She said, "Are you just going to do this for eight hours? Touch the clothes?"

I said, "I'll probably sit on the bench outside in a little bit. Maybe come back inside later. I like being here, you know?"

Victoria came to pick her up. Camilla got into the front seat.

I leaned in through Camilla's window. I asked, "What are

you going to do?"

Victoria said, "I'm going to take her to get a B-12 shot, and then we're going for a hike in Runyon Canyon." She added, hoping I said no I assumed, "You wanna come?"

I said, "I can't."

Victoria looked relieved. She said, "Why not?"

I said, "I have to be here."

Victoria said, "Why?"

Camilla looked at Victoria and shook her head, like, "Don't even ask."

Victoria said, "Also, I thought of something this morning — did you go to the New York Supreme store before you left? It doesn't seem like the trip would be complete if you didn't go to that one."

I said, "I don't think I am welcome in the New York Supreme store."

Victoria asked, "Why not?"

I said, "I wrote a blog post for *The New Yorker's* website about a store in the basement of a mall in Chinatown, in New York. The store resells Supreme merchandise that the owner buys at Supreme. And when it sells out at Supreme, he resells it for a lot more than he paid for it. And the blog post was popular, within the world of men's fashion I guess, and the people who work at Supreme saw it, and then–"

Camilla asked, "Is it legal to do that?"

I said, "Why wouldn't it be? They buy it and resell it fair and square."

Camilla tried to think of a reason, but there was none.

Victoria asked, "How does the article make you unwelcome at the Supreme store?"

I said, "The last time I went in to Supreme, the manager came out and said, 'Are you the kid who wrote that article?' I was like, 'What article?' I probably started sweating when he came over to me. I knew what was happening. There was probably a puddle forming at my feet. And then he was like,

'That article fucked with the store.' I said, 'Why? I thought it was complimentary of the store and the brand.' He goes, 'You wrote that we keep sold out stuff in the back for our friends? And now every fucking kid comes in here and is like, 'Yo, you got that sold out shit in the back? I know you do.' It's such a fucking hassle.' And then the manager escorted me to the door. I left and never came back. I knew they didn't want me there. And I didn't want to find out what they would do if I tried to come back."

Victoria said, "Do you write about anything besides Supreme?"

I said, "I tried to write a play before I went back to school. But I didn't finish."

CHAPTER XIII

I sat on the bench outside Supreme for a long time. I left some eBay feedback. Five stars all around, even when they waited three days to ship. I'm not a confrontational guy. I'd never found 'standing up for myself' to be a profitable activity, like any other form of complaining.

I thought about my play. It was about a skateboarder who gradually broke into every apartment in his apartment building by climbing in through the windows from the fire escape in the alley behind the building. He installed tiny surveillance cameras in other apartments and monitored the camera feeds from his computer. And then, when people left their apartments, he went into them and stole things to sell on eBay. The rest of the time, he just skateboarded. And then a neighbor caught him. I didn't know what would happen after that, or if it should end. I thought they could sleep together, but I couldn't come up with a natural series of events that would end in them sleeping together. But I thought it could have been a good play.

I thought to myself, "I am a loser, have always been a loser, and will always be one." I thought that would be a good title for my play, but it had nothing to do with the play.

CHAPTER XIV

In the afternoon, the store filled up with skaters. I sat on the bench outside and smoked.

I went back inside and looked through all of the merchandise again. I bought two packs of Supreme-branded Post-It Notes for $2 each. They were selling on eBay for $18 each.

I noticed that the guy working behind the counter was the white kid from Odd Future. I couldn't remember his name. He gave me a curious look. He must have noticed me sitting outside the store for four hours.

He said, "Do you need a bag?"

I said, "No, it's okay. It's just Post-It Notes." I put them into my jacket pocket.

I walked back outside and sat back down on the bench. I lit one.

I texted Camilla, "The guy behind the counter is the white kid from Odd Future. I just bought some Post-Its from him".

I Googled "white kid odd future" and looked through some pictures of him. He changed his hairstyle from blonde to black. Looked cool either way.

Camilla texted back, "Thought he looked familiar".

I walked over to Canter's to use the bathroom. I got a pastrami sandwich on rye bread with mustard and I ate it in a booth by myself. I slipped an Ativan into the sandwich and ate it like when a dog owner makes a dog take its medicine by mixing it in with its food.

I went into the bathroom, walked into a stall, and drank some vodka out of my bag. I took 5 milligrams of Mellow Yellow and 10 milligrams of Propranalol.

I walked back to Supreme and sat outside again. The sun was bright. I bought a pair of sunglasses from the white kid in Odd Future.

He came outside and swept away all of the cigarette butts I dropped on the sidewalk around where I sat. I lifted my feet so he could sweep. Two teenagers recognized him and went up to him and had him take a selfie with them. He was holding the broom. He gave a look like he would like to be anywhere else on Earth. Disaffected.

Some store employees came outside and stood around smoking. I listened to their conversation. They talked about where to go skateboarding. One skateboarded up and down the block, falling constantly, sometimes hitting his head. He came over to the group and said, "Skateboarding and thinking don't work together."

Another store employee came outside and started talking quietly to a man in his 50's who wore a dirty military-style jacket and neon green Nike running shoes. His name was Ernie. He was gaunt, especially in his face, like a lifelong smoker or an AIDS victim. I thought, "Do you become an AIDS victim when you contract the disease? Or only when it kills you?" I'd only heard the term "cancer victim" applied to someone who had died.

The gaunt man said to the Supreme employee, "How was your New Years?"

The employee said, "Oh, I kept it real low-key."

They made a hand-to-hand exchange, heroin I think, and the employee went inside.

At the end of the day, I texted Camilla, "Hey, can you come pick me up? And the car? NBD if not. I just don't think I should drive right now and the store is closing. If you're busy, I could just walk around until I'm fit to drive".

Victoria and Camilla came back to pick me up. I leaned into the car again.

I asked, "How was the B12 shot?"

Camilla said, "Very relaxing." She looked at my face. "But probably not as relaxing as whatever you're on."

I got into the front seat of Victoria's car and Camilla

followed us home in the rental car.

Victoria said, "What got you into Supreme?"

I said, "When we were in college, my girlfriend cheated on me with a guy who worked there. I found a Supreme shirt stuffed behind her bed. It was too big. I was like, 'What is this shirt? I've never seen you wear this.' I put it on and I noticed it smelled like B.O. in the armpits. So I figured the brand might have something to offer that I didn't then possess."

She said, "That's sad. I'm sorry."

We sat in the car for a while, passing diners and donut places that reminded me of *Pulp Fiction.*

I said, "I like the aesthetic here. Like, all the old diners and donut places. It looks so 1960's. All the storefronts in New York keep changing, but here, it seems like once they get something right, they keep it around for 50 or 60 years."

Victoria nodded.

She said, "Did it work?"

I said, "Did what work?"

Victoria said, "Wearing Supreme stuff. Like, in terms of getting whatever you thought you were going to get out of it."

I shrugged.

She said, in a coquettish tone, *"Do the ladies just love it, Dave?"*

I said, "Not really."

CHAPTER XV

In the morning, I woke up from a sex dream about Victoria. And then Camilla took me to get a B12 shot. It felt therapeutic. I exhaled.

I said, "This is probably what intravenous heroin feels like."

I went back to Supreme and sat outside all day again. Around lunchtime, I bought some more Post-It Notes. Same thing, the day after that.

We drove to LAX, dropped off the rental car, and went through airport security. I turned $1,000 into Japanese yen, bought 10 mini bottles of Smirnoff at the Duty Free shop, and the plane took off.

I looked down at Los Angeles and the Valley. I thought of some of the things I could have done there if I hadn't sat on a bench in front of Supreme the whole time I was there. I thought, "But there will be more time for that later in life."

I watched the new *Godzilla* remake on the in-flight entertainment system while I worked on the 10 mini bottles of Smirnoff. I drank 7 bottles.

Camilla pulled my headphones off my ears and whispered, "You smell like booze. If I had an alcoholic father or uncle, how you smell would bring back horrible memories of them."

I said, "Good thing you don't."

She said, "You said you wouldn't get that drunk again on this trip. Like you were on the first night."

I said, "What's the difference? I'm just gonna pass out anyway. It's not like we're going to talk through this 12-hour flight. And I'm not gonna, like, be a drunk and belligerent passenger."

Camilla said, "How do you know?"

I said, "It's not in my nature."

Camilla sighed. I put my headphones back on and went back to watching *Godzilla*. Most of it took place in Japan.

After the alcohol set in, I could no longer follow the plot of the movie. I took my headphones off and just sat there, waiting to fall asleep, moving at 550 m.p.h. over the Pacific Ocean to the other side of the world. It felt profound to think about, but I knew it didn't mean anything. Just a plane flying.

Camilla tapped me on the shoulder and whispered in my ear, "Can I tell you about a term I'm trying to coin?"

I said, "What do you mean?"

She said, "Like, a phrase I am trying to popularize."

I said, "How are you trying to popularize it?"

She said, "Just by saying it, hoping it'll catch on."

I said, "I think you need a public platform for that. It would take forever to catch on organically."

She said, "Can I just tell you what it is?"

I said, "What about Vine? You could say it on Vine and hope people repost it. If it's short enough."

She sighed and said, "The phrase is 'dip it in ranch.' Ranch dressing."

I said, "What does it mean?"

She said, "It means, like, 'go fuck yourself.'"

I said, "Like, 'Go suck an egg'?"

She nodded.

I said, "So if you didn't like someone, you could say, "Man, that guy is an asshole. He can go dip it in ranch'?"

She said, "Or, 'I wish Chelsea Handler would dip it in ranch already. She's not funny anymore.'"

I said, "I like Chelsea Handler."

Camilla said, "Do you like 'dip it in ranch'?"

I said, "I think it could catch on. What's the 'it' supposed to be? A penis? Like 'Suck it'?"

Camilla said, "'It' is not literal. It doesn't have to be anything specific."

I said, "But the ranch part is literal. It makes you imagine dipping something in ranch. People might hear it and think of a piece of celery. It wouldn't carry the same weight as 'Go fuck yourself' or even 'Go suck an egg.'"

Camilla said, "People will understand."

I said, "Can I tell you about a phrase I would like to popularize?"

Camilla said, "No."

I said, "Okay, so, you know, 'Does a bear shit in the woods?'"

Camilla said, "I've heard that."

I continued, "Or, 'Is the Pope Catholic?' Or, 'Is a frog's asshole watertight?' They mean, like, 'Yeah, duh.'"

Camilla said, "I know."

I continued, "Like, if you asked me, 'David, are you plagued by feelings of worthlessness and failure 100% of the time?' And I would say, 'Does a bear shit in the woods?'"

Camilla rolled her eyes. She said, "I know. I already said I'd heard that before. Except the frog one. But those phrases are already popular. Except the frog one."

I said, "I know. But here's mine – I mean, I read it online but would claim it as my own – 'Does Dolly Parton sleep on her back?'"

Camilla thought about this for a second.

She said, "That's good."

I said, "It's *really* good."

I put my headphones back on and opened bottle number 8. She pulled my headphones down. I liked when she touched me.

She said, "But Dolly Parton could sleep on her side, couldn't she?"

CHAPTER XVI

I couldn't sleep on the plane. When we got to Japan, I felt frustrated with myself for not being able to fall asleep.

I said to Camilla, "Can you collect our bags from the baggage claim? And meet me outside? I need a cigarette. I feel irritable. If I don't have a cigarette, I'm going to be a crabby baby. And I have to go to the bathroom. I'll collect the bags next time."

I went to the bathroom. The toilet was embedded in the ground. I took a picture of it, logged on to the airport Wi-Fi, and sent it to my mom with the message, "Arrived safely in Japan."

I looked at the toilet for a while and thought about how to crap in it. High risk of getting it on my pants accidentally. I Googled pictures of people crapping into Japanese-style in-ground toilets. It was hard to get the search language right. I found some pictures of people squatting in a certain way. Made sense. I crapped. What an arrival.

I walked out of the airport and lit one on the sidewalk near the pick-up and drop-off area of the terminal. I thought of The *Simpsons* episode where they fly to Japan and the pilot says over the loudspeaker, "Welcome to Japan. The local time is… tomorrow."

I smoked my cigarette. I looked around and people were giving me curious looks. I thought, "I'm American, they probably don't see that many Americans. They can look at me all they want. Maybe they think I'm on a TV show or something."

But then I noticed that the rest of the people smoking were standing inside a glass box a few feet away from me, and there were No Smoking signs posted all over. So I had to smoke inside this punitive box, I guess. I put my cigarette out and returned the remaining portion to my pack.

The smoking box had glass sliding doors. I didn't see a handle or anything. I waved my hands in front of what looked like a sensor but nothing happened.

A woman walked past me. I tapped her on the shoulder and said, "Do you know how I can get inside this box?"

She looked puzzled. She took out a pack of cigarettes and offered me one.

I said, "Oh, no, I have, thank you." I took out my own pack and opened it to show her that I had cigarettes. She didn't understand English.

I tapped my chest and then pointed inside the box. She tapped a panel on the door, the thing I thought was a motion sensor, and it opened.

There wasn't much space. I stood elbow-to-elbow, packed into a glass box with Japanese people smoking. I was the tallest person inside the box. The other people inhaled deeply, like they were trying to suck the life out. In the middle of the box, two loud aspirators vacuumed the smoke up. I wondered, "What happens to the smoke?" I didn't think the smoke was spewed out above us, because otherwise, what would be the point of having the smoking box at all? They're trying to prevent the smoke from being released into the atmosphere. I guess someone cleaned the aspirators. I felt claustrophobic.

Camilla came out of the airport and saw me smoking in the glass box. I waved to her. She laughed. I finished my cigarette and came back out.

Camilla said, "How was it?"

I said, "Worst cigarette I've ever smoked. The smoking boxes are only at the airport, right?"

Camilla said, "Oh, no, those are popular here. In most cities, it's illegal to smoke on the street, so you have to smoke in those."

I said, "You're fucking kidding."

She said, "I'm fucking not. *You* thought Bloomberg and Giuliani were bad."

CHAPTER XVII

We took a two-hour train into Tokyo, the cleanest train I'd ever been on.

I said, "I feel like I could eat off the fucking floor of this."

She said, "Don't."

Outside of the train station in Tokyo, there was a line of taxis. I tried to open the door of an empty one and Camilla said, "Don't do that!"

I said, "Why not?"

The door popped open.

She said, "It's rude. The taxi drivers are like chauffeurs."

The driver got out and put our bags in the trunk. I said, "Domo arigato."

Camilla laughed. I said, "What's funny?"

She said, "No one says, 'domo.' It's just arigato."

I joked, "What about, 'Mr. Roboto'?"

Camilla didn't laugh. That wasn't a good one. It was obvious. A little float in the parade of disappointments that started when I was born.

We got to the Airbnb, on the top floor of a high-rise in a neighborhood called Shinjuku. The club neighborhood, according to a guidebook. Our host was a middle-aged Japanese man with a gravelly voice. It sounded like he ate cigarettes. "Eating cigarettes" to describe a gravelly voice is from something, but I can't remember what. Not creative.

Our host made us put on slippers and led us to a small room.

Outside of the room was a big red light in the wall, which I guess would start flashing when there was an earthquake or nuclear disaster.

He said, "First time Japan?"

I nodded. Camilla held up two fingers because it was her second time. The host nodded.

I said, "Is there Wi-Fi here?"

He smiled and took out a folded sheet of paper from his pocket and handed it to me.

He said, "Americans are first ask: Wi-Fi? Wi-Fi? Wi-Fi?"

The host bowed to us and left the room. I bowed to him but he didn't see. We stood there with our bags at our feet. I looked around and out the window, down a long avenue of high-rises.

I said, "Where are the beds? Are there, like, murphy beds?" I looked around the walls to see if there were any panels that might be pulled down to reveal murphy beds.

Camilla opened a closet door and pulled out two mats and some blankets.

I said, "We sleep on those? On the floor? I hate sleeping on the floor. They don't have beds here?"

She shook her head.

I said, "Jesus Christ…"

She said, "They don't have him either."

Camilla made her bed while I stood on the balcony next to our room, smoking and drinking vodka. I came back inside and she said, "I'm exhausted. I have to go to sleep."

I said, "It's only 9:15! If we go to sleep now, we're just kicking the jetlag can down the road. I say we stay up as late as possible, party hard, sleep in until an hour before Supreme opens, and then we'll be on Japanese time."

Camilla said, "Nope. And we're also not going to spend our whole time in Japan at Supreme."

Camilla brushed her teeth in the bathroom, changed into her t-shirt and underwear, turned the light off in the room, and got onto her bed mat.

I rolled my mat out next to hers and got under my blanket. We both lay on our backs, looking up at the ceiling.

I said, "I don't think I'm tired. And my back hurts. I don't like sleeping on the floor. I feel hyper."

She said, "I'm tired. Don't be a baby."

I said, "Can I tell you another thing from the Talmud? Now that Victoria isn't here. I promise it has nothing to do with rape."

She said, "You're trying to piss me off, right?"

I said, "The Talmud has rules designed to make marriages last. The first thing is a rule called the Family Purity Rule – it says that a man can't have sex with his wife from the first day she gets her period until a week after it's over. That means, like, half the time, married couples can't have sex. And not only that – they can't even touch each other's hands or even sit close to each other on the couch. She can't even pass him the salt. And if they're not sure her period is over, the woman can take a sample on a tissue and send it to a rabbinical authority for analysis."

Camilla said, "What about other women besides his wife?"

I said, "No way. That's, like, in the Ten Commandments. You don't even need the Talmud for that. 'Thou shalt not covet another man's wife.'"

Camilla said, "What about a woman who isn't another man's wife?"

I said, "No, you can't even covet another man's maidservant or even his ox."

Camilla said, "What if she's not another man's maidservant? Like, *not affiliated with another man at all.* Can you imagine?"

I said, "Then she would be, like, owned by her father."

Camilla said, "Oh, cool."

I said, "Hey, I didn't write it. And fathers owning daughters is whatever compared to the rest of the bone-chilling shit in the Bible."

Camilla said, "Is there more to this magical system to keep marriages together?"

I said, "The second thing is a rule that says men can't waste things. It doesn't explicitly say 'no masturbation,' but by masturbating, a man would be wasting his sperm. So it's interpreted that way."

Camilla said, "What about women?"

I said, "Women can waste all they want. I don't know why. So men can't use condoms, but women can use diaphragms. *Women* can waste a man's sperm. That's how Orthodox Jews do birth control, as a side note. With diaphragms and stuff."

Camilla said, "How does this help marriages?"

I said, "Sexual desire fades over time. That's a truth of human existence. And so –"

Camilla rolled her eyes. She said, "Is it?"

I said, "Couples just get bored, like 'the seven-year itch.' But with this system, because husbands and wives can't have sex half the time, and men can't ever masturbate, half the time in a marriage, the couple, especially the man, is rebuilding desire. It keeps desire going for much longer and probably makes the sex better too, because it never becomes, like, once-a-week obligation sex."

Camilla shrugged.

I said, "No one has sexual fantasies about their own wife, I think, except probably people who follow the Family Purity Rule. Like, when people masturbate, it seems like they think about people they aren't regularly having sex with."

Camilla said, "You've never masturbated to your own girlfriends? I think women would be saddened to hear what you're saying if it's true for all or most men. I sort of assumed my boyfriends were masturbating to me when we weren't together."

I didn't say anything.

Camilla said, "I guess that sounds naïve when I say it out loud…"

I said, "I don't really masturbate. And, yeah, sadly, I don't think they were masturbating to you. But can you see how the Family Purity Rule is designed to keep sex in a marriage interesting for longer? Like, how it sounds 'just crazy enough to work'?"

Camilla said, "You don't masturbate?"

I said, "Not really."

She said, "Have you ever?"

I said, "Yeah, when I was in high school. It just wasn't for me."

Camilla said, "Isn't that like saying, 'Food – it just isn't for me'? Isn't that abnormal for men?"

I said, "It saps my motivation. There's a whole subreddit about this. If I masturbate in the morning, it's like I'm on lithium for most of the day. And if I go, like, a week without doing it, I feel like I'm on a low dose of Adderall all the time. It's like free drugs. And it makes me feel proud that I have some discipline and self-restraint. And I don't have to imagine what I look like when I'm doing it, like a monkey in a zoo. You know? Have you seen a man sitting in a computer chair and masturbating? It's pathetic. There are, like, products I don't even want to consume because masturbators love them."

Camilla said, "Like what?"

I said, "Mountain Dew. Xbox."

Camilla said, "Do other people know you don't masturbate?"

I said, "Like, among our friends from school? Or in society?"

She said, "Either."

I said, "I don't think so. I don't, like, advertise it. I assume other non-masturbators don't advertise it either. I know people think it's weird, and not in a cool way."

Camilla said, "Do you enforce the Family Purity Rule in your relationships?"

I said, "Good one. 'Enforce.' I can't even enforce finishing a movie she's suggested we watch in my relationships. I haven't ever proposed it, but maybe I'll suggest it to my wife when I'm older."

Camilla said, "I like your presumption that someone would marry you."

Camilla fell asleep. I watched *The Simpsons* on my phone.

CHAPTER XVIII

When I woke up, I felt rested. I stretched my arms out. I looked out the window and although the sun wasn't out yet, I figured it was probably just before dawn. I looked at my phone to check the time. It was 1:09 a.m. I tried to fall back asleep for a few minutes, but I couldn't.

I Googled "Tokyo club zone," realized it was only a few blocks away, and took a screenshot of the neighborhood on Google Maps with a pin at my current location. I got up and drank the rest of my vodka.

I walked down the street into Tokyo, towards the club zone.

I thought, "I could do anything I want here and nobody in my life would ever know. I could go to a strip club or have sex with a prostitute. I could address people by ethnic slurs." But no one would think anything of it but me.

I walked through Shinjuku, the club neighborhood. All of the bars and clubs were on high floors of high-rise buildings. I stopped at a 7/11. I didn't know it existed in Japan. I bought Japanese Marlboros with a plastic mirror on the front of the pack, some Suntory Whiskey, and some triangles of rice. They were wrapped in seaweed with chopped fish inside.

As I checked out, I pointed to the whiskey and then pointed outside to the street and put a puzzled look on my face, to ask the woman behind the counter if it was okay to drink on the street. She nodded at me.

I walked down the street for an hour, sipping the whiskey from my jacket pocket and eating the triangle rice snacks. I bought a can of beer from a vending machine and drank it.

I walked past groups of drunken Japanese people, going from one club to another. They didn't notice me. I passed mostly parking lots, batting cages, and convenience stores. There was no street parking.

When I finished the rice snacks, I smoked one. It was light, so I smoked another. I figured if a cop stopped me for smoking on the street, I could just say, "I don't speak Japanese, I couldn't read the signs, I didn't know it was illegal," and he'd probably let me go. I was a guest in his country.

I wandered back to the high-rise district, looking for another 7/11 for a bag of shrimp chips.

CHAPTER XIX

On a brightly lit street full of clubgoers, a man who looked Moroccan, wearing a leather jacket, came up behind me and leaned in to my ear. He said, "Sex, sex!" He was the first non-Japanese person I'd seen since the airport. He spoke with an accent I'd never heard: half from a country in Africa or the Middle East that I couldn't identify, half Japanese.

I stopped. I was surprised to be acknowledged. I hadn't had sex in a long time. I thought about his offer. But if I had sex under those circumstances, it would have made me an Asian Sex Tourist. Not so far from a child molester.

I said, "I'm cool, thanks anyway." I kept walking.

He followed me. He said, "What girls you like?"

I ignored him and took out another cigarette.

He said, "Gay? You are gay?"

I kept walking. He was following me.

He said, "What girls you like?" again.

I said, "Girls who live in South Brooklyn and work at newspapers and magazines in Manhattan."

He looked confused. He didn't have any of those girls on tap.

I said, "Media types." It was lost on him but worth it to me. I could tell someone else about it later.

I started walking again and he walked next to me.

He said, "Come on. Girls. Open your heart to me, man."

I said, "I'm good."

He said, "You are good without a girl?"

I nodded and walked faster. I went into an arcade where Japanese people were trying to win plush animals from claw crane game machines. I thought, "Those are rigged, right? That's the consensus on those machines? Claw crane game machines?"

I walked around the arcade a few times, sipping my whiskey, hoping that when I came out, he'd have found a new mark. I found the bathroom and crushed a half an Ativan and put it under my tongue. It was bitter. "A bitter pill to swallow." I got it now.

I came back outside and he was smoking a cigarette. He looked at me.

I said, "I'm just not interested. I promise you, dude, you're wasting your time. There is nothing you can say to get me to have sex tonight."

He opened his arms, looked up, and said, "Look around yourself! Shinjuku! You came to the sex."

He followed me again. I didn't feel threatened because there were plenty of people around and he was pleading with me. And Camilla told me there was no crime in Japan.

He said, "Why you came Shinjuku?"

I remembered passing a batting cage.

I said, "For the batting cages."

He looked confused.

I said, "Baseball," and swung my arms through the air like I was holding a baseball bat.

I turned around and walked back in the direction of the last batting cage I passed. I realized it seemed suspicious because I was going in the other direction, but it was the best thing I could come up with.

He walked behind me in the direction of the batting cage.

He said, "Baseball and then beautiful girl, right?"

I said, "Only baseball."

He laughed like he didn't believe me, like it was an absurd thing to say, like he was wearing down my resistance, and we kept walking. I put my headphones in and didn't put any music on. I got to the batting cage five minutes later. He was behind me.

I said, "What are you doing?"

He said, "Baseball."

He swung an imaginary bat through the air and looked up and then slowly back down, like he was watching his home run fall into the stands.

I wondered if there was something wrong with him. He was probably wondering the same thing about me.

I walked into the batting cage building, which looked like a bowling alley. He was behind me. I couldn't read any of the signage. There were 20 cages, most of them being used by people who seemed to be taking a break between nightclubs. They were dressed up.

There were no non-Japanese people around and it didn't look like there ever had been.

I walked into one cage. There were bats on the ground and a machine to put money in. It said "300 yen," which was about $3. I took my jacket off and dropped it on the ground and took some money out.

I picked my bat. The pimp started putting money into my machine.

I said, "No way, dude. There is no way I am getting into your debt." I didn't think he understood my words exactly, but he knew what I meant.

I took out a 100 yen coin from my pocket, which is what the machine said he had already put in, and put it into his hand. I put the other 200 yen into the machine and a bell rang. He got out of my batting cage and stood behind it. He put his fingers through the fence and looked at me. Like a dad at a Little League game.

The balls came flying at me fast, probably like 65 mph. I

missed the first few and tipped the next few. After about ten, I hit my first one, weakly. The force of the ball almost knocked the bat out of my hand. I gripped it harder.

I looked back. A few Japanese people had gathered behind my batting cage. I guess they were expecting to see an American excel at his national pastime, like Paul Bunyan. ¯_(ツ)_/¯.

But then I hit the last 3 balls, out of my 20, squarely. I was getting it.

I put another 300 yen into the machine and went again. I felt humiliated by this pimp, angry and alone. I wished Camilla was there. I tried to smash one and I missed, and then I tried again. And then… "Thwack!" The sound of the bat hitting the ball.

But then I missed two. But then "Thwack! Thwack!" And I missed one. And then, "Thwack! Thwack! Thwack!" I thought of my girlfriend who cheated on me. Fuck her, "Thwack!" Camilla sleeping instead of coming out with me. Fuck her too, "Thwack!"

I thought of George W. Bush's fucking monkey face. What a fuck he was. "Thwack!" My parents fighting in the living room, "Thwack!" The first doctor who thought it was a good idea to give me Ativan, "Thwack!" Fuck him too. All the doctors who keep giving me this stuff, "Thwack!" The sources of my fucking problems!

The two years I wasted after college trying to be a professional writer, "THWACK! THWACK!" My friends who succeeded, "Thwack! Thwack! Thwack!"

The balls ran out.

Another 300 yen. "Thwack! Thwack!" The guy who fucking sold me a water-damaged iPhone 5 on eBay and then deleted his account and disappeared, "Thwack!" The white guy from Odd Future who didn't even try to talk to me after I sat outside his store for three days, "Thwack!"

Climate change deniers, "Thwack!" The pimp gawking

at me, "Thwack!" Every single thing I read on the internet, "Thwack!"

My second 20 balls were out.

I went over to my jacket and took another sip of whiskey. I looked down the row of cages. Japanese people, drunker than I was, dressed meticulously, some even wearing suits, nailing every ball. What a fucking country.

I put another 300 yen in and missed the first six or seven balls. I'd lost my rhythm. I put my bat down, picked up my jacket, and walked out of the cages and onto the street.

I lit another one. The pimp came out behind me and lit one.

He said, "Sex? *Beautiful* girl."

I screamed, "Fuck you, dude! Just leave me the fuck alone!"

He put his hands up, with his palms towards me, defensively, as if to say, "Who, me? I wasn't trying to do anything."

I turned around and walked again. This time, he didn't follow me. I made sure I had my wallet.

For a few blocks, I walked. I was stumbling. I drank too much again. I could barely stand up. I didn't know where I was going. I looked at the screenshot on my phone to try to make sense of it, but all of the text was in Japanese.

I walked back towards the batting cage, the only familiar place around. When I got there, I walked forty feet down an alley between the batting cage and a parking lot.

I lay down and curled up in a corner against the wall, behind some garbage cans at the end of the alley. I put my headphones in. I put my hood on. I fell asleep to music.

CHAPTER XX

I woke up around dawn. An employee of the batting cage tossed a bag of trash on me. It was sealed, so nothing spilled. The sun was coming up.

I groaned in surprise and he heard it. He hadn't seen me when he threw it. I stood up and tried to remember where I was and figure out why I'd been hit with a bag of garbage. I was in a fugue. My glasses were crooked on my face and there was drool on my cheek.

I looked at the batting cage employee who threw the trash on me. He stood there frozen, with such a look of such terror and remorse on his face that I'll never forget it.

I tried to smile but my lips were stuck together with dried spit. I was drunk. I opened my eyes wide and shook my head, like to say, "Really, it's fine. Not a big deal."

I put my tongue through my lips.

I said, "Dude, it's totally fine. Nothing got on me. No liquids or anything. And I shouldn't have been sleeping there. You didn't even know I was there! It's cool. It's completely my fault."

I tapped my chest to signal that I was responsible.

I said, "My fault."

He came closer to me and said some stuff in Japanese that I don't understand, but it sounded remorseful. He bowed.

He would have let me keep sleeping there if I'd wanted to,

but I was cold. I thought, "I should go back to the Airbnb."

I said, "No, really, we're good, it's all good," as he continued to apologize in Japanese. We walked together out of the alley towards the street.

I took out my phone and showed him the map of the neighborhood, with the pin where my Airbnb was. He gave me directions, as best he could, with his hands. He took the phone and held it in front of us and pointed in each direction, and then pointed at the map, orienting me.

I bowed to him. He bowed and apologized again in Japanese, I think, and said some other remorseful-sounding stuff I didn't understand. I got the gist. I stumbled home.

CHAPTER XXI

I took off my shirt and pants, put my coat back on because it was cold in the room, and slept next to Camilla.

In the afternoon, she woke me up. She gave me a rice triangle that she bought at 7/11 while I was sleeping.

She said, "You look like fucking shit. Why are you sleeping in your coat?"

I said, "I was cold. Let's go to Supreme."

CHAPTER XXII

We walked down through Tokyo to Supreme Harajuku, stopping to pick up whiskey. I didn't even feel like drinking it, but I couldn't resist drinking on the street given the opportunity.

We took pictures of each other in front of the Japanese Communist Party Central Headquarters. It was a beautiful building. Groups of conservative-looking Japanese men in suits walked in and out.

I said, "Can you imagine the American Communist Party Central Headquarters?"

She smiled. She said, "Yeah, it's probably on the 6th Floor of the shittiest building on, like, 29th and Broadway. The buzzer doesn't work."

I laughed. I said, "And everyone inside is a 53-year-old guy, bald on top, with a gray ponytail."

Camilla smiled.

We passed a lot of stores and buildings featuring peculiar English or nonsense portmanteaus. Stores called "Freak's Store" and "RAGEBLUE," next to each other, sold clothes that wouldn't look out of place at J. Crew.

A sign outside of a restaurant that was closed said, "CLOSED (sorry we're)."

Another store was called Wafflish Waffle.

In Harajuku, there was a luxury apartment building that

said HARAJUKU LIVIN' on it.

Almost every street corner had a vending machine on it. Camilla sipped a bottle of hot tea from a vending machine.

A lot of people were wearing hats and backpacks with the New York Yankees logo. A woman walked past me wearing a hoodie that said "NEW YORK" in small letters and then, below that in much bigger letters, "FULL OF BEANS".

As we got close to the Supreme Harajuku store, my heart raced. I attributed it to excitement but then realized it was because I hadn't taken any sedatives that day. It was hard to tell which of the things I was addicted to was the source of my discomfort.

I tried to remember when I last took each of my pills. I bit a Mellow Yellow in half and put the other half back in my pocket. I took an Ativan. I smoked one. I felt okay.

When we turned on to the street Supreme was on, I said to Camilla, "We're almost there, holy fuck."

She said, "How do you know? I don't see it?"

I said, "I've been up and down this street on Google Maps. I know where all the Supreme stores are by sight because I've been to them on Google Maps."

We walked into Supreme Harajuku. I thumbed through all of the merchandise carefully. The prices were higher than they were in America. A pair of chinos for $118 in the US was equivalent in yen of $230.

Camilla trailed me and picked out a long-sleeve t-shirt with a picture of a stallion on the back. She held it up to her chest.

I said, "You should get that. The image is the first thing that comes up when you Google Image Search the word 'stallion.'"

She said, "That's funny."

I said, "Probably not to the guy who took the picture."

She said, "This is illegal? I feel so 'rebellious.'"

I said, "The picture is from, like, HotWallPapers.com. I don't think HotWallPapers saw any money from the Supreme stallion shirt."

She bought the stallion shirt.

Behind the counter, I found the carabiner that had a secret compartment to store pills in. It was Japan-only, the holy grail of Supreme. I bought five.

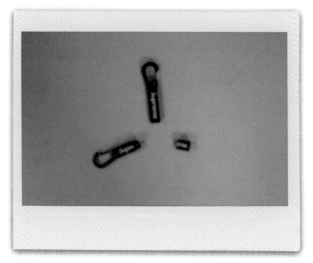

Camilla said, "So this one is pretty much exactly like the one in LA."

I said, "To you, maybe."

She said, "I guess I didn't realize, even in LA, that you were going around the world to go to exactly the same store nine times. I thought they'd be different in Japan."

I said, "The layouts are different. The music is different. Like, all King James bibles aren't the same. They might all have the same text, but some are bigger. Some have gilded edges. Et cetera."

She said, "These stores are *really, really* similar."

We left for Supreme Shibuya and walked through Harajuku.

Camilla said, "What are you planning to do with five of the little keychain things you bought?"

I said, "They're not just keychains – they store pills secretly. But, I don't know, maybe sell them? They were like $15 each and they might go on eBay in America for like $50 or $100 because they're Japan-only. But I'll probably keep them. Eventually, they'll wind up in a box in the basement of my house. I'll open the box in like 30 years and think, 'Wow, I remember when I thought these pill carabiners were the coolest

things on Earth.' And my wife will be like, 'What's Supreme?'
And I'll be like, 'A thing from earlier in my life.'"

We walked in silence for a few minutes. I said, "Can I tell
you something about Supreme accessories?"

She said, "Only if you give me one of your little pill things."

I said, "Nope."

She said, "Okay, you can tell me anyway. But you have to
let me bore you equivalently later."

I said, "Deal. I have a theory that what unites Supreme's
accessories is that most of them have some sort of illicit/
underworld connotation having to do with violence or drugs.
But they appear, for the most part, ostensibly innocent – only
when viewed together do you get the sense that they're sug-
gesting something illicit."

I thought about this for a second.

I said, "The pill carabiner keychain is obvious – conceal
your drugs. The only kind of pill buyer who doesn't have a
bottle to carry their pills around in is someone who buys their
pills in baggies. But there are so many others. Like last season,
they made this little plastic case with a company that makes
cases to keep valuables dry during water activities, like kaya-
king. But it can also be used as an airtight container to keep
your marijuana fresh.

"They also make lighters with Zippo and Bic."

Camilla said, "To light your 'marijuana' with, I presume?"

I said, "Yes. This season, they made a keychain that looks like a .44 bullet, but it's actually a small knife. Like, a little knife pops out of the top of the hollow bullet shell.

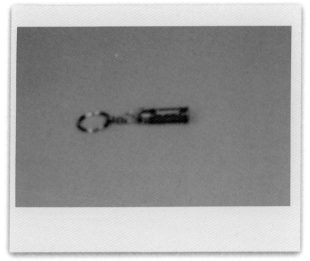

"They've made boxcutters,

"A hollow Bible,

"And last season, they made a youth baseball bat with Mizuno.

"Ostensibly, it's for, like, teaching your five-year-old to take his first swings. But it would be useful in an armed robbery – a small bat would probably get the job done just as well as a big bat, but it's easier to conceal and carry. And also carries a lower legal penalty than using a gun."

Camilla said, "And owning these accessories makes you feel rebellious and dangerous?"

I said, "Of course. My favorite one from this season is the Supreme toothpicks."

Camilla said, "How could toothpicks possibly be illicit?"

I said, "You know how in mafia movies, there are always tough guys standing around, chewing toothpicks? And in Westerns, too? Tough guys chewing toothpicks with mean glints in their eyes? Chewing a toothpick has an underworld connotation. Goons chew toothpicks. Something menacing about a guy chewing a toothpick, in the right context. Like, compare it to bubble gum. Or a soda straw."

Camilla said, "I'm not sold."

I said, "Imagine you bring a boyfriend home to meet your parents. And you want him to be on best behavior. But he shows up chewing a toothpick. You'd be like, 'Take that fucking toothpick out of your mouth, you're meeting my father. You look like you work at an auto body shop.'"

Camilla shrugged.

She said, "I'm hungry."

I said, "Let's stop at 7/11. We're burning daylight."

She said, "You can't come all the way around the world and just go to 7 fucking 11."

I said, "Of course I can. I love 7/11. And it's different here."

She said, "How is it different?"

I said, "They don't have Slurpees. That's, like, the core product. And the fucking sushi."

Camilla said, "I'm not eating every meal in Japan at 7/11. I'm just not. You can eat there if you want to. I'm going somewhere else."

My will was overborne. We ate in an American-themed restaurant. I got a steak and eggs. It was served with a side of rice, like everything else in Japan. Best steak and eggs I'd ever eaten.

CHAPTER XXIII

We walked to Supreme Shibuya. It was distinguished from all others by a large blue statue of a Sphinx sitting in the center of the store. The employees wouldn't let us take a picture of it. One of them stood in front of it with his arms folded when I tried.

I touched all of the clothes again. I bought the shirt with the stallion on it even though I had two already. Because it was sold out in America.

Camilla said, "Don't you already have that?"

I said, "Not in this color."

She said, "Did you ever consider that you have, like, a Freudian collector thing going on?"

I said, "What do you mean? Like I collect Supreme because I subconsciously want to stuff it up my ass?"

She said, "Stop playing dumb."

I said, "I'm not playing dumb."

She said, "Only someone dramatically overconfident in their intellect could say all the knowingly dumb things you say."

I said, "Well, the more things you learn in life, the more you realize you don't know."

She said, "You didn't learn about Freud in high school?"

I said, "We didn't dwell on the discredited stuff. Freud, leeches, flat Earth, phrenology, stuff like that."

Camilla said, "Leeches aren't discredited – they use them now for skin grafts, you fucking smartass."

I said, "Did you know cigarettes lower your risk of Parkinson's disease?"

Camilla said, "That sounds like bullshit. It's probably because smokers die earlier. That's like saying 'smoking lowers your risk of dying of natural causes.'"

I said, "No, I swear, it's independent of that. I read it on a science blog. Same thing with cholesterol. Smoking lowers your cholesterol."

Camilla said, "You don't read science blogs."

I said, "I do when, like, BuzzFeed links to them."

Camilla sighed and said, "I think you have a Freudian collector thing going on with Supreme."

I said, "I pay you out of pocket for this analysis? Or you bill my insurance?"

Camilla said, "Fuck you. Freud said that people collect things as a way of channeling their surplus libidos into objects of desire. Sounds like you're a prime candidate."

I said, "Because I don't masturbate?"

Camilla said, smirking, "No, because you have a totally

normal, healthy sex life."

She looked at me for a second. "Of course because you don't masturbate!"

I said, "Maybe I should just masturbate and we can get the next plane out of here."

Camilla looked wounded. Like I suggested I didn't enjoy being with her. She straightened her face.

She said, "Fine. Go jerk off. I'll change our flights."

I said, "But we've already paid for all the Airbnbs, right?"

She didn't say anything. She looked a little wounded again. I'd won because I'd gotten her to make a facial expression that revealed that she liked being around me. I lit one.

CHAPTER XXIV

We walked to Supreme Daikanyama, the last of three Supreme stores in the city of Tokyo. It was a small store. Camilla bought a pink hat that referenced the Sweet'N Low logo.

We walked back to our neighborhood to have dinner with a Japanese woman Camilla spent one semester with during a foreign exchange program at her high school.

On the way, Camilla said, "Don't ask them any offensive questions about Japan. I will be so embarrassed."

I said, "How am I supposed to know what's offensive or not? I don't know the culture here. I don't know what they would be offended by. I bet I could say the n-word all night and Japanese people wouldn't know the difference. How am I supposed to know?"

Camilla looked straight ahead. She didn't say anything.

I said, "Like, if we go into the restaurant and I don't take my shoes off, will I have offended your friend and all of her ancestors or something?"

Camilla said, "David?"

I said, "What?"

Camilla said, "Dip it in ranch."

We met Camilla's friend on a corner. Her name was Mariko. She had straight teeth and her hair smelled perfect. I could smell her shampoo. I should have found out what kind it was, bought it, and left it in the bathroom for my girlfriend to use the next time I had one.

I couldn't stop looking at her. I imagined taking her back to the Airbnb to sleep with her while Camilla occupied herself somehow. The batting cage or something. But there was no clear route to that.

Once, I read an account by a female-to-male transgender man about going on the hormones that gave him a man's body. He wrote that the most notable mental effect of the hormones was that he started having pornographic thoughts about women he passed on the street. He was shocked. I thought to myself, "Women didn't have these thoughts also?"

Mariko brought her co-worker. I didn't catch his name. He was a short guy dressed in a tailored suit, carrying a briefcase. We all walked to an authentic Japanese restaurant Mariko picked. Nothing on the menu was in English.

At the table, Camilla and Mariko talked about high school and me and her co-worker glanced at each other. He had a stern face. I needed a drink. I suspected that she invited her co-worker because he spoke English. They didn't seem to have a warm rapport.

I asked, "How old are you?"

He said, "26."

I said, "Sick, me too."

He said, "What is 'sick' about it?"

I was just making conversation. I tried to think of something to say.

I said, "Well, it's the last year of the mid-twenties. That's, like, the prime of life – old enough to have learned a few things, young enough so that the body isn't failing at all. I can still drink like I could when I was 19. But then, next year I'll be in the late twenties, and then, like, I don't know? My back will probably start to hurt or something. And I'll be ready to move into the next phase of my life, which I'm not ready for."

He sat there, staring at me. I think I was joking. I don't know. He didn't seem to think I was joking. He took a sip of his water and looked around over my shoulder. I didn't know what to say, but I didn't want to horn in on Camilla's conversation, which didn't pertain to me.

I said, "What do you do?"

He said, "Civil engineering."

I said, "That's, like, designing bridges and stuff?"

He nodded and said, "Yes, 'and stuff.'"

He sighed.

He said, "What do you do?"

I said, "I'm still in school."

He said, "What makes you come to Japan?"

I said, "There's this men's clothing brand Supreme, and we're on a trip to all of their stores in the world. And Japan has six."

He said, "How many are there in total?"

I said, "Nine – London, Los Angeles, and New York are the others."

He said, "It's a Japanese brand?"

I said, "No, it's a New York brand."

He said, "Why so many stores in Japan?"

I said, "There's an appetite for good design, here, I think. Supreme could put a store in Dubai or something, but they like tacky shit there, as I understand it. Supreme's idiom would be lost on the people there."

He said, "What do you mean 'lost'?"

I said, "It's hard to explain."

He said, "They do formalwear?"

I said, "Mostly casual clothes. Sometimes they sell suits, but they're leisure suits. Nothing you could wear to work."

At the table behind him, I saw a man smoking.

I said, "Am I allowed to smoke in here?"

The co-worker said, "Yes, but we're non-smokers."

I lit one. He looked at me with distaste.

I thought he meant, "Yes. But we're non-smokers. But go for it anyway." But then I understood he actually meant, "Yes, but we're non-smokers, so consider that when determining whether to smoke around us."

¯_(ツ)_/¯.

I looked at him and said, "Smoke 'em inside if you got 'em."

He nodded.

I said, "In New York, it's illegal to smoke in restaurants, and to drink on the street, so in Japan, I like to take these liberties."

Mariko ordered for the table.

Mariko said, "I just ordered a stew for us. It's amazing here."

I said, "Sweet. I like stew."

Mariko said, "How do you like Japan so far? It's your first time here, right?"

I said, "Yeah, it's my first time. It's really cool. So civilized and clean. And people are polite and elegantly dressed. No super fat people. In fact, no fat people at all. Not that I have any personal problem with fat people, but, I guess, having a ton of fat people means society is fucked up somehow. Putting too much pressure on people. Driving people crazy. I don't know how to articulate it better, but does that make sense?"

Mariko shrugged.

I said, "And everyone takes pride in what they do. Like, today I used the bathroom in a McDonald's and it was cleaner than any public bathroom I've ever been in in America. It was cleaner than the bathroom in my apartment. Even the cashiers at the convenience stores, like, hand you your receipt with two hands. It makes me feel like a barbarian."

I continued, "So it's a super tight country. I mean, in my opinion."

Mariko smiled.

Camilla looked uncomfortable and said to Mariko, "Can we get some sake or something?"

Mariko nodded and flagged down the waiter. She ordered sake for the table.

I said, "And everyone is Japanese here. I guess, living in America, I thought multiculturalism had really bled into the rest of the world, and globalization and whatever. And every country was at least a little diverse. But in Japan, like, everyone is still Japanese. I walked around Shinjuku for like three hours last night and didn't see a single non-Japanese person, as far as I could tell. Except this one guy who looked like he was from Morocco."

She said, "Was he trying to get you to come into a club?"

I said, "Sort of." I thought for a second about telling her the story, but it ended with me sleeping on the street. She wouldn't want to sleep with a guy who'd spent the last night sleeping on the street.

I said, "Being here makes me remember that, like, America is an experiment in putting people who don't look alike or share the same values in the same country. You know? But then, like, the white people hate the black people and the brown people, and the black and brown people in turn hate the white people."

I bumped my fists together for emphasis.

I said, "But in Japan, you couldn't be like, 'I hate all these people – they're all conniving, greedy cheapskates with hook noses, beady eyes, and overbearing mothers, and they control the media,' or something like that, you know? Because everyone's, you know, Japanese. You'd have to hate everyone. It feels like everyone's on the same team here."

Her co-worker said, "What about Japanese people? In America? Do people hate them?"

I said, "I guess Asian people are sort of on the sidelines of the hate game. Except when they crowd white people out at prestigious colleges, and then the white people try to make it harder for them to get in."

Camilla kicked my foot.

I looked at her and said, "Am I being ignorant?"

She said, "You're doing your best to sum up an infinitely complex situation. Do you want to ask them things about Japan instead of trying to explain America?"

Mariko laughed nervously.

I said, "Sure! Okay, I thought of this one when we were at the airport – is there still an emperor?"

Mariko nodded.

I said, "Are there weird free speech restrictions here? If I walked up to a cop and said, 'Fuck the emperor,' would, like, I go to jail or something?"

The co-worker laughed. He said, "No – it's pretty much the same as in America."

I pointed to Camilla and said, "She said that there's no crime here. Is that true?"

The co-worker said, "For the most part. There are some crimes that are unreported, but in general, yeah, there is not so much 'street crime.'"

He thought for a second.

He said, "When there is a street crime, Japanese people assume that a non-Japanese person committed it. Maybe a Chinese laborer? Or a tourist?"

Mariko said, "Generally, the attitude among Japanese is that Japanese simply do not commit crimes. Except the Yakuza."

I said, "That's like what Ahmadinajad said! He was the President of Iran, and when a reporter asked him about gay rights, he was like, 'Homosexuality? We don't have that in Iran.'"

Camilla said, "The Yakuza is the mafia?"

The co-worker said, "Yes."

Camilla turned to me. She said, "That's why you can't have tattoos here! Because only the Yakuza have tattoos. When I came here last year with my sister, I couldn't go into the public baths because of my tattoo."

I asked, "What's your tattoo? I didn't know you had a tattoo."

Camilla said, "A chameleon. It's the logo of my Dad's boarding school."

She started to lift up her pant leg. Mariko looked at her nervously. She put it back down.

I said, "Okay, I have another question – what's up with the English here? It doesn't seem like many people speak English, but almost all of the stores have their signs in English. And people wear a lot of clothing with English lettering on it."

Camilla's friend said, "Yeah, it doesn't really have to do with what the words mean – English is... cosmopolitan. People in Japan think imported things, especially from America, are better than Japanese things."

I said, "I feel like you, as someone who speaks perfect English, could walk down the street all day and think, like, 30% of the things you pass are sort of funny. Like, I passed someone wearing a shirt today that just said, 'I Am Thinking Big.'"

She said, "It fades after a while, but sometimes I notice. We saw someone wearing a baseball cap that said 'Bad Party' on it on the way to dinner. We thought that was funny."

I asked, "When you're on the bullet train, does it really *feel* like you're going 200 mph? Like, impossibly fast? And you're, like, pinned to the wall on the curves or something?"

Mariko said, "When you're on a plane, going 500 mph, does it *feel* like you're going 500 mph? Or is it smooth?"

I said, "I see." What a stupid question.

Camilla looked at me like it was time to stop asking questions.

I said, "Okay, fine, here's my last one: Is the sushi at 7/11 actually good? Or is it the worst sushi in Japan, but better than most of the sushi in America, so I don't realize it's the worst sushi in Japan?"

Camilla glared at me. She didn't want my theory confirmed.

The co-worker said, "It is good. Even to the Japanese. The stores have no storage space, because space is very expensive in Japan, so they get fresh deliveries over and over during the day."

I said, "And because people take pride in what they do here, right? Like no self-respecting store in Japan would sell shitty sushi? Right? Or shitty anything? It's a cultural thing, right?"

Mariko shrugged.

I looked at Camilla like, "I told you!"

I said to Camilla, "See? I told you it was fucking good."

CHAPTER XXV

Camilla and I walked home through Shinjuku, the club district. None of the pimps came up to me because I was with a woman.

I said, "Do you think they thought it was like *Dinner with Schmucks?* Where I was the schmuck?"

Camilla said, "I don't think so – you sounded ignorant, but like you were aware of your own ignorance. Like, in a good-natured way. You presented yourself as a curious ignoramus, I thought. To the best of your ability."

I said, "Should we get fucked up before we go home?"

Camilla said, "I'm really tired."

I said, "But it's 9:30!"

Camilla said, "Exactly."

I said, "Can I get fucked up on the way home?"

Camilla sighed. She said, "Just watch yourself."

I took a bottle of whiskey out of my backpack.

It was a small bottle, so I drank the whole thing. I tossed it into a recycling bin next to one of the tea/coffee/soda vending machines because there were no public garbage cans in Japan. I forgot to ask about that.

We got back to the Airbnb. We got into our beds, on the floor next to each other, and turned the lights off.

Camilla said, "Are you really drunk?"

I said, "I'm not sure what you mean by 'really.'"

Camilla said, "When you get this drunk, it makes me feel alone."

I leaned my head against her shoulder. I nuzzled her shoulder with the top of my head.

I said, "Do you want a Mellow Yellow? To fall asleep."

Camilla said, "What's the downside?"

I said, "It makes you want to cry."

She thought about it for a while and then turned it down.

I said, "I love to cry."

We lay there. I rubbed my head against her shoulder again. It was tender. She was letting me have a tender moment. I was going to remember it. She stroked my hair with her hand.

I said, "Can you give me a haircut?"

Camilla said, "I've never given someone a haircut."

I said, "I'll shave my head if you fuck it up."

Camilla shrugged. I got scissors and whiskey out of my suitcase and we went into the bathroom. I took my shirt off and sat on the toilet. I sipped the whiskey. I liked when she touched me. I would use any excuse. The hair fell on my shoulders, onto my back, and down onto the bathroom floor. She blew lightly on the back of my neck to get the hair away. It felt so good to me.

CHAPTER XXVI

In the afternoon, I woke up in the bathtub with vomit on my face. Good thing I'd taken my shirt off for the haircut. I turned the water on with my foot.

We walked to the Meguro Parasite Museum, a museum of parasites. I ate another piece of fried chicken and a sausage on a stick.

I said, "I've only eaten rice, fish, and fried shit since we got here. The diet is terrible. I don't know how these people stay so thin."

Camilla said, "I haven't seen anyone else eating fried chicken and drinking whiskey on the street. Maybe that's part of it. Why don't you get a salad?"

I said, "Have you seen a single salad on the menu at any of the places we've eaten so far? There are no salads in this country."

Camilla said, "Did you know 'salad' used to refer to only mayonnaise-based salads? Like 'tuna salad' or 'egg salad'? It's only recently that salad means, like, lettuce and tomatoes and carrots and stuff. 'Green salad,' it's called, in the rest of the world."

I said, "How recently?"

She said, "The 1960's? In America. Was the advent of 'green salad.' Maybe it hasn't happened here yet."

I shrugged.

Camilla said, "Also, 'salad' just means 'an unstructured mishmash of shit.'"

I said, "Aren't most foods unstructured mishmashes of shit?"

Camilla said, "No. Most foods have structure. Think about it – pizza is bread on the bottom, then sauce, then cheese on top. If you made it with the cheese on the bottom and the bread on the top, I don't know what you'd have, but it wouldn't be a fucking pizza."

I thought about this for a second. She was right. It would not be a pizza.

She said, "And salad's sister is soup – a salad is an unstructured mishmash of *dry* shit and a soup is an unstructured mishmash of wet shit. That's why entrees are eaten with 'a side of soup or salad.' You get some structured food and a mishmash of unstructured food, wet or dry, as you like it. And something to wash it down with. That's a meal."

I said, "I like that."

For a while, we didn't talk.

I said, "Have you noticed how quiet it is here? Like, walking down side streets? No music coming out of cars, no one talking in their apartments with windows open and it spills out onto the street. No jackhammering, no clanking from trucks. It's eerie."

Camilla said, "It's the workday – people are at work."

I said, "But it's true, like, even in restaurants. People speak quietly. Everything is quiet."

Camilla said, "I see what you're saying."

I said, "The only areas that are loud are the ones with the tourists."

At the Parasite Museum, there was no staff: no guards, no guides, no attendants, no one giving out information at the front desk. In the front room, there was a small "suggested donation" box. I put 500 yen, about $5, into the box.

We walked through the museum, looking at all of the different parasites that have infected humans, animals, and plants. Nematodes, maggots, worms.

There was a turtle in a jar whose eye had been replaced by a parasite that ate it and then stayed in the eye socket until a scientist put the whole thing into a jar.

The museum was full of silent Japanese people. Some held hands. Most took photographs of the parasites. The only sound in the museum was the sound of the cell phone cameras' shutters, because it's illegal in Japan to sell a cell phone or camera that can take pictures silently, or have the shutter sound disabled, because of the popularity of upskirt photography. Some Japanese people looked at my iPhone with their heads tilted as I took photos with the shutter sound off.

I whispered to Camilla, "Do you want to go upstairs?"

She looked like she was going to vomit. She said, "Not really."

Upstairs, in a jar, was the world's longest tapeworm. Next to it was a length of rope that you could stretch out to get a sense of exactly how long the tapeworm was. Eight feet.

A few feet away from that was a photograph of a man, shot from behind, who ingested some sort of parasite. The parasite had colonized his penis and made it huge. In the photo, he was walking down a dusty road. His penis dragged along the ground.

I went back downstairs to get Camilla. She was waiting on a bench to leave.

I whispered, "Hey, can you come upstairs? There's a photo of a huge penis. I feel like I'm inside Reddit. It's fucking amazing."

Camilla came upstairs, looked at the photo of the penis, and gagged. We left.

We walked through Tokyo. I lit one. I said, "I bet, like, the third day after the guy got the parasite, he was like, 'Fuck yeah! I got a huge penis now.' I bet his wife was like, 'I can't believe my good fortune!' But then it just kept growing."

CHAPTER XXVII

I ate another piece of fried chicken from 7/11 as we walked to a bunny café. It was the only place Camilla wanted to go.

We sat on the floor of the bunny café and Camilla stroked a brown bunny.

I watched a news report about the *Charlie Hebdo* shooting on a television hanging on the wall behind Camilla. I don't know why they didn't have children's programming on. They kept playing the cell phone footage where one of the jihadists executes a police officer as he's laying down in the street. He's yelling "Allahu Akbar!"

I went into the bathroom and drank some vodka. I took an Ativan and a Mellow Yellow.

Camilla ordered a 150 yen (~$1.50) bowl of vegetables to feed to her bunny. There were some little girls at the bunny café, but they were more focused on playing with their bunnies than watching the *Charlie Hebdo* street shootout. Camilla was too. I understood. She looked so happy, smiling like a little girl, stroking the bunny and looking into its eyes and laughing.

I started sneezing. I think I was allergic to those bunnies. But I didn't say anything. I kept this in my back pocket for the next time Camilla said I was being selfish, so I could bring it up then.

Camilla started crying. I stood up and walked over to her

and sat down next to her and rubbed her back and whispered, "Why are you crying?"

She sobbed. The little girls looked at us and then looked back at their bunnies. They didn't say anything.

I said, "What's wrong?"

She kept crying. The tears ran down her cheeks. She wiped them away with her sleeve.

I said, "We don't have to talk about it. Communicate it to the bunny and he can debrief me after."

Camilla smiled.

She said, "I don't know why."

I said, "Is it about the bunny?"

Camilla shook her head.

I said, "Nothing at all to do with the bunny?"

She shook her head again.

I said, "Do you not want to talk about it?"

Camilla shrugged. I turned around and they were playing the execution again.

I thought about the next thing I was going to say for a long time. I sat in silence for about ten seconds as Camilla wept next to me and little girls giggled behind us.

I said, "Are you getting your period?"

Camilla laughed. She stopped sobbing.

She said, "You're such a fucking asshole."

I waited a few seconds.

I said, "But are you?"

She didn't say anything, just kept stroking the bunny. She flared her nostrils at the bunny, mimicking it. The bunny flared its nostrils. She fed it a carrot.

I said, "You could fit everything I know about women into a thimble, but that's one of the things I know."

Camilla said, "That women get emotional about 'nothing' when we're getting our periods?"

I nodded. I said, "Not 'nothing.' But less than usual."

She looked down at the bunny. I didn't know what she

was thinking.

And then she looked me in the eye for a moment and nodded.

A tear stopped moving down her cheek.

She said, "You're right. I hate that you're right."

Her eyes were all puffy.

I wiped a tear off her cheek with my thumb.

I said, "Can I play with it for a second?"

I picked up a piece of lettuce and held it in front of the bunny.

CHAPTER XXVIII

We walked to a coffee shop called "Geek's Coffee." According to the sign, it was a coffee shop "for coffee geeks." I needed to find the bathroom. I walked up to the counter, took out my phone, opened the Notes app, and typed in the toilet emoji. And then a question mark. I showed it to the guy behind the counter. He pointed me towards the bathroom.

I went into the bathroom to take a Propranalol while Camilla got a cup of coffee. There was a sign above the toilet with a bulleted list:

- SELECT YOUR COFFEE AND DRIP ON HOW YOU FEEL TODAY.
- CHAT WITH OUR STAFF TO FIND THE COFFEE THAT'S BEST FOR YOU.
- APPRECIATE YOUR COFFEE WITH A SMILE BEFORE DRINKING.
- IF YOU FIND SOMEONES' BOOKMARK, LEAVE IT IN PLACE.
- TRY THEM ALL. YOU'LL FIND YOUR OWN.
- HEARTBREAK TASTES LIKE BITTER COFFEE.
- RETURNING THE MUG BACK ON THE SHELF IS THE "GEEK'S" WAY.
- FIND THE RESTROOM AT THE FAR END, LEFT OF THE ENTRANCE. ONE CUP, UNLIMITED ACCESS.

I came out and said, "They're really into coffee here."

Camilla said, "Yeah, it's a tea culture. All they had was tea for like 10,000 years. So coffee seems exotic and imported, I guess, like she was saying the other night."

We took the train three hundred and two miles west to Osaka. My first time on the bullet train. The front of the train looked like a dolphin.

I put a full cup of coffee on a small tray that extended out from the bottom of the window. Even as we were going 200 miles an hour, the coffee didn't spill on me. Not even a drop.

I said to Camilla, "When Mariko compared the bullet train to an airplane at dinner, I should have pointed out that an airplane might not feel fast because you're five miles off the ground."

Camilla shrugged.

I drank some of the coffee and poured some vodka into the cup when there was space.

I ate another piece of fried chicken, which I had been saving in my backpack.

Camilla said, "You're getting fat."

I said, "You mean since college?"

She said, "Well, yes, since college. But that's over years. But I meant on this trip. You look like you've gained five or ten pounds."

I said, "It's probably because my face is bloated. I haven't been sober since the morning we left."

Camilla said, "Even through the bloated face."

I said, "I'm actually going bald, too."

Camilla said, "No, you're not. That's just in your head."

I said, "The problem is that it's not in my head. All the hair I used to have, I mean. Rimshot."

Camilla said, "Why do you make corny jokes like that? Just because a joke can be made doesn't mean it has to be."

I said, "Why do you have to point out my flaws? We're on vacation."

Camilla says said "Because you can control this one. And

no one else is going to tell you."

I shrugged. I said, "Can I show you my disappearing hair in the mirror in the bathroom?"

She said, "You think we can just leave all our stuff unattended?"

I said, "It's Japan. We could leave $5,000 in cash on our seats and go to the bathroom for half an hour and no one would touch it. Maybe someone would pick it up and bring it to the lost and found."

We walked to the bathroom. I lifted up the hair that covered the spaces next to my widow's peak.

Camilla said, "You've always had a widow's peak. Even in college. That's just your hairline."

I said, "No, I know, but it's thinner around the widow's peak. I never used to be able to see my scalp. I used to have a full head of hair. Now, I can see little parts of my scalp."

Camilla examined it and looked like she saw what I was saying.

She said, "I have seen hair in the shower on this trip... But I thought it was just natural shedding?"

I said, "I thought it was natural shedding too, until, like, I noticed my hair was getting thinner."

We walked back to our seats and sat down.

I said, "It makes me want to get married now, before I lose it all, and then become a less appealing marital property."

She rolled her eyes.

I continued, "Like, in the marriage market where every potential partner is weighing every other potential partner's attributes collectively, like looks, money, family, personality, history of mental illness, etc. Once my hair falls out, my stock will go down."

Camilla said, "You think of marriage like that? Like, with every partner as a bundle of attributes whose value you calculate?"

I said, "Human life is bleak."

Camilla said, "Thinking about it that way makes it even bleaker."

I said, "Doesn't everyone think of marriage like that? Even if not consciously? Not to shatter your impression of marriage as between two people who just fall in love and say fuck everything else. I mean, it's not that conscious. I don't sit there with spreadsheets and stuff."

Camilla said, "I don't think the kind of woman who would considering marrying you would care about your hair once she finds out about your personality."

I said, "You only say that a woman wouldn't care about my hair loss because you're more attractive as a woman than I am as a man. So you wouldn't be marrying me for my looks anyway. So you assume no woman would marry me for my looks. But a woman who is just as attractive as a woman as I am as a man, or less attractive, would value my looks. This marginal category of women is the group I am concerned will not want to marry me once my hair falls out."

Camilla said, "You think I'm attractive?"

I said, "Yeah. Like, objectively. But after almost a decade of knowing you, it doesn't register to me. You just look how you look. Do you know what I'm saying? Like, if a woman just as attractive as you walked down the street, I would think, like, 'That's an attractive woman right there,' but with you, it doesn't cross my mind. Swear to god." What else could I say?

Camilla said, in a tone I couldn't understand, "That's nice to hear."

CHAPTER XXIX

We got to the Airbnb in Osaka. Our host was a 29-year-old English man who appeared to be playing video games on his TV when we walked in.

We introduced ourselves and put our stuff down in the bedroom.

Camilla said, "I'm going to take a nap."

I went back out into the living room.

I said, "Is it okay if I sit down?"

Our host nodded. I sat a few feet away from him on the couch.

I said, "What game is this?"

He said, "Super Metroid."

He had an accent I'd never heard: an English accent with a Japanese accent creeping in, like he hadn't spoken English in a long time.

He wasn't holding a video game controller.

I said, "Are you playing?"

He said, "No, watching. It's a championship."

I said, "I didn't know you could watch other people play video games. Are these people professionals? Like, professional video game players? I saw a *New York Times* story about a professional video game player, but I couldn't read it. You know, ten free articles?"

He didn't say anything. He was watching the video game.

I said, "I didn't know there were audiences."

He said, "How would they be professionals if there were no audiences?"

I said, "I assumed they just made bets with each other. Like, 'If I beat you, you give me $5,000.' Like online poker."

He said, "That would be professional gambling, not professional gaming."

He took a piece of pizza out of a Costco pizza box in front of him. I didn't know there was Costco in Japan. We sat there for a few seconds, watching people play video games on TV. I guess I was bothering him.

I said, "I didn't know they had Costco here."

He said, "What are you doing in Osaka?"

I explained our Supreme trip.

He seemed curious. He said, "I've passed that store. Never been inside, though."

I showed him, on his iPad, a small Supreme shopping bag on eBay for $20. To give him an idea of the cult of Supreme.

He said, "Just the shopping bag? Do you have to pay for it at the store?"

I said, "No, it's free. They put your stuff in it when you buy stuff."

He said, "Wow."

I said, "Do you want to go? I mean, after the championship."

He shrugged and looked at me. He said, "We can go now. This is a marathon. It'll be on when we get back."

CHAPTER XXX

I walked through Osaka with the English Airbnb host.

He said, "I came to Japan to teach English after college, found another job after that, met my girlfriend, and then I just never left."

I said, "Do you like living here?"

He said, "It's isolating. People here don't respect Westerners. There's a word for it – gaijin. It means foreigner. It's derisive."

I said, "Oh, I remember that word. From *The Fast and the Furious: Tokyo Drift.*"

He said, "When I speak Japanese here, peoples' mouths drop. They just assume all foreigners don't speak Japanese, aren't curious about Japanese culture, and have come to fuck their women."

He seemed resentful about that last thing. I didn't say anything.

He said, "The internet speeds are fast. Really fast. Second-fastest in the world after South Korea."

I said, "That's sick."

He said, "Yeah."

We walked for a while without saying anything. I couldn't think of anything else to talk about and he was comfortable with silence. Luckily, I thought of something.

I said, "What language do you think in?"

He said, "Depends on who I'm talking to. If I'm talking to someone in Japanese, I think in Japanese, but if I'm talking to someone in English, English."

I said, "What if you're not talking to anyone?"

He said, "Depends on the situation, like the stimulus. If I'm on the subway here and the ads are Japanese, I think in Japanese. If I'm on the street in London, English."

I said, "What if there are no stimuli? Just, like, laying in bed at night with the lights off, waiting to fall asleep?"

He said, "Probably Japanese."

I said, "Have you thought about moving back to England?"

He said, "I've thought about it, but, like, what's there for me now? I haven't lived there in a decade. All of my friends have professional jobs, wives, some have kids. I wouldn't know where to start."

We got closer to Supreme. I explained some of my theories about the brand, including the underworld accessories theory and the intentionally unsalable clothing theory.

He said, "Have you considered that it's just a bunch of guys who put things they think are cool on t-shirts and skate-boards? And then people like you develop elaborate theories about why they are cool? But there may just be nothing there beyond people putting things they think are cool on t-shirts?"

I said, "I've considered that. But I guess it's like really religious people – they must wonder, sometimes, whether God is real, right? Like, if you've dedicated your life to serving God by being a monk, you must wonder, at least *occasionally*, whether God is real, right? Or if the whole thing is bogus? And there's no proof for it, so they just choose to believe it's real, because life would be meaningless if it wasn't."

He said, "But your life wouldn't be meaningless if this Supreme brand was just guys putting things they thought were cool on t-shirts. You aren't a monk for Supreme."

I said, "I have a lot of eggs in this basket."

He smiled.

He said, "Where else are you going in Japan?"

I said, "We're thinking about going to Kyoto next. There's no Supreme store there, but my traveling companion said it's worth checking out. All the temples and stuff. She was there last year with her sister. I told her I don't give a shit about Shintoism, but she still thinks it's worth seeing. What do you think?"

He said, "The thing about the temples here is that once you've experienced one, you've experienced them all. It's like the people."

CHAPTER XXXI

At Supreme, I touched all of the clothes again. The Airbnb host seemed intrigued by a t-shirt. He looked at it for a while.

I said, "Could I ask you a favor?"

He said, "Maybe."

I pleaded, "Would you be able to ask one of the employees here a question in Japanese? I'm curious about what they like about Supreme, or, like, what they see in it."

We went up to the counter. My host asked the question in Japanese and the guy behind the counter answered. My host turned to me.

He said, "He said, 'I think Supreme, some day, could be like Ralph Lauren.'"

I said, "Can he elaborate?"

My host turned and asked the question. The employee answered.

He said, "He said that Supreme makes good clothes, they've made them for a long time, and they have a consistent aesthetic."

I must have had a puzzled look on my face. My host said, "I'll explain when we walk home."

I said, "Can I ask another question? This might be sort of a stretch."

My host nodded.

I said, "Can you ask him, like, where he parties? Or, like, where people who work at Supreme party? Or, like, where they will be partying tonight?"

The Airbnb host turned and asked the question and said a lot of stuff in Japanese. He talked for 30 seconds. I didn't understand what he was saying. The Supreme employee behind the counter laughed. He took out a Supreme business card and wrote an address on it. They said more things back and forth in Japanese.

We walked out of the store.

When we get onto the street, I said, "Thank you. Wow, fuck. This is awesome. I can't believe this. I'm gonna get to see these guys in their natural element."

For the first time, my host looked at me like I wasn't bothering him.

He said, "No problem. I can understand where you're coming from. Like, you're obsessed with this. There's a word for it in Japanese – 'otaku.' It means, like, nerd. And it doesn't matter what other people think – it's just part of who you are. I feel the same way about gaming – like, some people might think whatever about watching professional gaming, but fuck them."

I nodded.

I said, "What was the thing you wanted to say after he said the Ralph Lauren thing?"

My host said, "Fashion means something different in Japan. Like, in America, or in England, fashion has some cultural connotation – a guy with dreadlocks and a beanie with the colors of the Jamaican flag is communicating that he's, like, a Rastafarian. Maybe that he smokes weed, you know? Sees the world in a certain way? Or, like, in England, a guy with dyed black hair in tight black jeans and a leather jacket with anarchy patches and pins all over it – that guy is a punk. And he hates Margaret Thatcher, or the state in general, or David Cameron or Conservatives. Like you – you wear skate shoes, baggy pants, a hoodie – you're, like, a 'slacker' or something. Or a hipster. Or you want to be seen as one, by communicating it through what you wear. You expose your ideology through your clothing."

I said, "How is that different in Japan?"

He said, "In Japan, clothing doesn't really have a cultural connotation the same way you think of it – here, if you see a guy with dreadlocks, it's because he thinks that's a cool hairstyle, not because he smokes a lot of weed. In fact, weed is illegal here. Like, they'll put you in jail. No one smokes weed here. You can barely get Tylenol. And if you see a guy dressed like a punk, it's unlikely that he actually, you know, is an anarchist or something. He thinks it's just a cool way to dress. So for these guys, Supreme and Ralph Lauren are somewhat interchangeable – Ralph Lauren might look like 'preppy American gear,' and Supreme would look like 'skater American gear,' but they're not thinking of it the same way – they think of it aesthetically, but the aesthetics don't *mean* anything."

I said, "What were you saying to him when you were talking for like 30 seconds?"

He said, "I told him you were going on a trip to every Supreme store in the world. He said you were otaku. He said, 'He can come to the bar.'"

We walked along for a while as I smoked.

The Airbnb host said, "People here aren't rebellious the same way. Skaters here wear Supreme, but skateboarding doesn't have the countercultural connotation it does in the US or the UK. It's just another thing to do, like running or biking. And so Supreme doesn't mean the same thing to people here as, I imagine, what it means to you. There is no counterculture. There is no political discord. A few weeks ago, the President proposed a major economic plan and the whole country was like, 'The leader thinks this is a good idea? Let's try it!' They just follow the leader."

I wasn't sure if he was right, but I guess he knew better than I did.

He said, "People here think, if something is wrong in their life, that it's their fault, not someone else's. Not the state's. They turn it inward."

I said, "Is that, like, the people who stay in their houses for years at a time?"

He said, "Yeah. Western-style rebelliousness is… Lost in translation."

We got back to his apartment. He went inside.

I wandered around the neighborhood.

I stopped at 7/11 and got a rice triangle and a piece of fried chicken and ate it on the street.

I found another 7/11 and bought a small whiskey and

drank half. I smoked three and felt uncomfortable, so I took an Ativan. I went back to the apartment.

The host was watching the video game championship on the couch. Camilla was still napping. I put on my Supreme Flower Pants. Soft cotton and covered in floral print. I crawled into bed beside her.

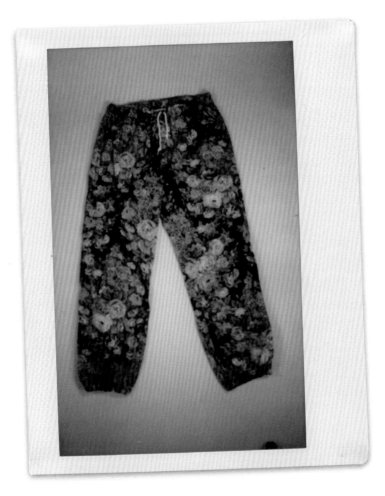

CHAPTER XXXII

We went to the bar whose address the Supreme employee wrote down. It was on the third floor of a building full of bars. Very remote from the street. We stood in the doorway. I scanned the faces of the people sitting in the bar.

There were fifteen Japanese skaters dressed in Supreme and Stüssy, sitting on couches or at long tables. A skater with a beautiful voice did karaoke to a schmaltzy ballad.

Half of the skaters appeared to have girlfriends, sitting next to them, generally dressed in clothing of the same brand as their boyfriends. The guys and their girls sat very close to each other. Everyone was smoking.

I scanned the room for the Supreme employee. I couldn't find him. Gradually, everyone turned and looked at us and stopped talking.

I whispered to Camilla, "I think they don't see many Americans in this bar."

Camilla whispered, "Y'all act like you've never seen a white person before, jaws all on the floor like Pam and Tommy just burst in the door."

I looked around. I said, "How do you know that by heart?"

She said, "It's only two lines."

I saw a guy sitting on a couch in the corner of the bar, next to a window, without a girl next to him. He looked at us like he recognized us.

He stood up and walked over to us.

He pointed at me and said, "Shpreme! You love?"

I took a second to recognize that he was saying Supreme. I nodded and smiled.

He pointed to himself and said, "Also, love Shpreme. I working in Shtüssy."

I reached out to shake his hand. I said, "I'm David." He shook my hand. He pointed to himself and said, "Shogo."

Camilla introduced herself. Shogo had trouble pronouncing her name. She said, "You can just call me C." He didn't understand. She pointed to herself and said, "C."

He looked at her and said, "C. C. C.," practicing.

I looked around again for the Supreme guy. I said, "Is the Supreme guy here? The guy who works at Supreme?"

He shook his head. He pointed to himself and said, "Shtüssy. Work Shtüssy."

I said, "Ah, cool, Stüssy."

He said, "You love Shtüssy?"

I don't care for Stüssy but I didn't want to offend him. Supreme or nothing. I said, "Oh, yeah, I love it."

He said, "Yes, cool."

I said, "Thanks for having us. This is really pretty much what I wanted to happen on a trip around the world to every Supreme store."

He looked at me like he was trying to piece it together. I realized that he understood maybe one or two words I'd said.

I said, "Arigato," and bowed, and he bowed back.

He beckoned to a guy sitting on a couch near him. The guy came over to us and said, "English. I study. I am friend Shogo. Our friend, work Shpreme, say you are coming. He say you go every Shpreme around the world. Otaku."

I said, "Sweet." We introduced ourselves to the translator. He was also wearing all Stüssy. I said, "Thanks for having us."

The translator told Shogo what I'd said. Shogo said something back. The translator said, "He says you are welcome."

I ordered a whiskey from the bar. I sat on a couch near Shogo, the translator, and a woman who appeared to be the translator's girlfriend based on how close together they were sitting.

Camilla went to the bar and ordered a beer for herself. She came back to where I was sitting.

She said, "Hey, can you get this? I don't have any cash."

I said, "Sure. I have like $40. That should be enough for a while. Just tell him to put it on my tab."

She nodded and went back to the bar, got her drink, and sat down on a couch across the room. She introduced herself to a couple and started drinking the beer. She wanted to make friends. I understood that.

I told Shogo and the translator where we were going on our trip, that we lived in Brooklyn, and asked them about themselves. The translator's girlfriend didn't say a word. When the translator didn't understand what I was saying, I typed emojis into my phone. But it got tiresome. I felt like I was playing charades. And it was impossible to exchange any non-benign information.

I walked over to Camilla. She was drinking a second beer and talking to people in similar charades.

I whispered, "I can't talk in charades anymore." We went to the bar. I ordered a shot of whiskey.

She said, "Go back and talk to them. Or, like, just listen to them. If you didn't try to talk so much, you wouldn't have to do the charades thing so much. Don't be rude."

The bartender put my shot down and Camilla picked it up and drank it. I ordered another one.

We went back to our respective seats. I talked to Shogo about American music. I talked to the translator about how English is different from Japanese. Who gave a shit. I felt like I was in a group exercise in my high school French class. "An exchange student comes to stay with your family…"

The skater doing karaoke was singing loud. I slid a little

closer to the translator on the couch so I didn't have to yell or lean in to his ear to speak.

Shogo reached into his back pocket and took out his iPhone because, I guess, no one was talking to him. As he reached back, it tugged his long sleeve up a little. I saw that he had a tattoo, two black bars, on his wrist.

I pointed to it and said, "Tattoo?"

He looked surprised. He didn't say anything.

I said, "I have a tattoo also." I pulled up my sleeve and showed him mine. "Fuck Bush". I'll never forgive him.

He smiled and lifted up his sleeve to his elbow. His forearm was covered.

He said, "In America, tattoo, is cool?"

I said, "Oh, yeah, super cool."

I said, to the translator to say to Shogo, "We heard that the only people who are in the Yakuza have tattoos. Is that true?"

The translator looked at me. He didn't even turn to Shogo. He shook his head.

I said, "Ah, okay. Good to know."

The translator nodded. And then he spoke to Shogo in Japanese for a while as I sat there. Something was wrong.

I looked for Camilla to bring her over to show Shogo her tattoo. She was sitting at the bar and drinking another beer. I came up to her and said, "Hey, the Stüssy guy has tattoos. And the translator says it *doesn't* mean he's in the Yakuza. Do you wanna show him your tattoo?"

Camilla said, "You asked them if they were in the Yakuza?"

I thought about this for a second.

She said, "Like, point blank?"

I said, "Not exactly?"

She said, "You're an idiot."

I said, "I guess I just figured it would be obvious that I'm cool with them being in the Yakuza. And, like, they wouldn't think I was a threat. Like, an undercover cop or something. Like, a cop wouldn't just *ask* if they were in the Yakuza."

Camilla sighed and took a drink. She leaned in close to my face and said, "Can we dance? I want to dance. I don't want to talk anymore. It's pointless." Her breath smelled like alcohol.

I said, "You can. You know I don't dance."

Camilla said, "Why not?"

I said, "I'll embarrass myself."

She just looked at me.

I said, "I can't dance. I'm a loser, have always been a loser, and will always be a loser. I just can't. I'll look like an idiot. You dance."

She said, "Who gives a fuck? We're fucking in Japan. You're never gonna see any of these people again."

I said, "I'll see you again."

I ordered a whiskey and water. I sat down on the couch with Shogo and the translator again.

They weren't smiling at me anymore. I thought, "I shouldn't have asked about the Yakuza."

I watched Camilla dancing by herself. She was an amazing dancer. She looked like she was in Saturday Night Fever. For the second or third time on this trip, she looked happy.

I smoked another one. In Japan, the cigarettes were categorized by milligrams of nicotine. An American Spirit blue had 16 milligrams. The Marlboros I bought had 1 milligram. I thought, "I could smoke those all night."

Shogo and the translator kept looking at my Flower Pants and at Camilla, dancing by herself. They were putting two and two together.

I felt embarrassed about the Flower Pants. They were meant to demonstrate confidence in my masculinity, but suddenly, it seemed like I was just a guy wearing very effeminate pants.

The karaoke singer started singing even louder. I slid very close to the translator on the couch to speak into his ear.

I said, "Do you have any tattoos?"

Shogo reached out and put my hand onto the translator's

knee. He started laughing. He said, "Gay? Gay?"

I laughed nervously and said, "No, I'm not gay."

Shogo pointed at me and the translator. Shogo laughed, and then he looked half-serious for a second, and then he laughed again.

The translator laughed too. He looked at me and pointed at his girlfriend with his thumb. He said, "My girlfriend."

I looked at the translator. I pointed to my pants and said "Supreme" to justify them in case these flamboyant pants were why they thought I was gay.

He looked at Shogo for confirmation that they were indeed Supreme. Shogo nodded and said, "Shpreme." Supreme has never made an article of women's clothing.

I pulled out another one and lit it.

Shogo pointed at me and said, "Kissing?" and then pointed at the translator. I didn't understand. He said, "You want kissing?" I realized it was because I was leaning in very close to the translator's ear to speak.

I slid away from the translator.

I pointed to my ears and then pointed to the speakers. I held my hands up and opened and closed my palms to signal that the singing was loud. He said something to Shogo in Japanese. They talked for a while. I knew they were talking about me. I didn't know what to do.

I finished my drink. I stood up and walked back to Camilla. I brought her to the bar.

I said, "There's something weird going on. They're making fun of me. Shogo and the translator just joked that I was gay, like a schoolyard taunt. It was weird. And then Shogo put my hand on the translator's knee and suggested I wanted to kiss him because I was leaning in to talk to him. Because it's loud in here."

Camilla said, "Why do they think you're gay?"

I said, "Because I'm wearing floral pants and I was leaning in to the translator's ear really close. And, like, I'm here with you. And we're not, like, boyfriend and girlfriend. So, like, what's the alternative?"

Camilla said, "What do you mean, 'What's the alternative'?"

I said, "What's the alternative to us being boyfriend and girlfriend? Like, in the minds of the people here. It's either we're dating or I'm gay and you're my friend."

Camilla said, "Why can't we just be two people who aren't dating?"

I said, "Because two heterosexual adults of the opposite sex traveling around the world for pleasure…? That's just, like, not a social configuration that exists in adult life."

Camilla said, "That's not true."

I said, "It is true. It's only because we met in college and became friends that we happen to now be two heterosexuals friends of the opposite sex traveling the world for pleasure. College is the last time this happens. But we're 26 now. Like, when was the last time you met a straight man who you had no work relationship with and became platonic friends with him? Probably, like, me, right?"

Camilla looked like she was trying to think of a person who fits this description.

I said, "Adults want only money and sex. The only reason our relationship is exempt is because it was frozen into the friendship paradigm in college, when straight people were making new friends of the opposite sex. But the people in this bar don't know that. And it would take like a half an hour to explain it."

Camilla looked around the bar and exhaled. She didn't say anything. She was frustrated.

I said, "I know what you're gonna say. You're gonna say, 'Dip it in ranch, David.' But I will not dip it in ranch. There's something ominous going on here."

Camilla said, "You're wrong. But I don't want to litigate this with you now. Why do you even give a shit if they think you're gay? It's not like we're in, like, Uganda. I bet we're within walking distance of a gay bar."

I said, "Because the Stüssy guy is probably a gang member. Because of the tattoos. And now he knows that I know."

Camilla said, "Let's pretend for a second that you didn't just tell me having tattoos doesn't necessarily mean you're in a gang – what does that have to do with it?"

I said, "Have you seen *The Sopranos?*"

Camilla said, "Yeah."

I said, "You remember the episode where Junior doesn't even want anyone to know that he goes down on women? Imagine if he was gay. They would kill him for sure. I mean, granted, he was in their gang, but, like… Gang members just don't like it. I don't know how Japanese gang members would react to an apparently homosexual American in their bar."

Camilla rolled her eyes. She picked up her drink and looked back at the dance floor.

She said, "We're fine. This is the safest country on the planet. You're being paranoid."

I said, "Probably."

I finished my drink. I signaled to the bartender to bring me the check with the check-in-the-air hand signal.

She said, "Do you want me to pretend to be your girlfriend?"

I said, "I would rather just go home. You stay. This isn't that fun."

Camilla pouted. She said, "Can we just have one decent night out? If you leave, I have to leave too."

I knew she was right.

I said, "You really wanna stay?"

Camilla nodded. She gave me a pleading look.

I said, "Okay, you can pretend to be my girlfriend."

Camilla looked relieved. She looked up at the ceiling. She said, "God, I don't know what I did to deserve the honor of pretending to be this dipshit's girlfriend so people don't think he's gay, but thank you."

I said, "You don't really think I'm a dipshit. You'll secretly like pretending to be my girlfriend."

Camilla rolled her eyes again. She kissed me on the cheek. She pulled away and looked at me. I guess I looked stunned.

She kissed me on the lips.

I felt a rush of uncomfortable feelings. It didn't feel good. It wasn't supposed to happen like this. As she kissed me, I just sat still. I just wanted to leave. She kissed me again. I thought, "Why didn't it feel good?" I didn't know.

I put my arm around her and rubbed her back. My arm was stiff like I'd never rubbed a back before.

I thought, "If this woman were my girlfriend, how would I be acting? I've had girlfriends before, I know how to do this."

Camilla took my hand and dragged me to the dance floor. She started dancing. I stood there.

I tried to dance – one foot, the other foot, my arms, my neck, moving in a rhythm. I had to think about every step. I hated dancing. I felt like I was at my Bar Mitzvah, dancing with my grandma. I knew the Japanese people around us were looking at me.

I whispered to Camilla, "Could you not be so good? I look like a fool."

Camilla danced slowly, looking at me, pleading with me to keep going.

I said, "I can't. But you should keep going."

I walked over to the bar and paid for our drinks. It left me with about $5.00 worth of yen. Almost nothing.

I took my drink and sat down at the bar. I waited for time to pass. Read half a *VICE* story on Pocket. Thought about killing myself. I went back over to Shogo and the translator. I told them Camilla was my girlfriend. I went back to the bar.

I thought about Camilla kissing me. That shouldn't have been how it happened.

I typed out responses to old emails on the Notepad to make it look like I was doing something productive and therefore had a reason to not talk to anyone. Always a lot happening on the phone for a busy guy like me.

I turned around and saw Camilla dancing with Shogo. I turned back, hoping they hadn't seen me. I was a cool guy, secure and easygoing enough to let another guy dance with my girlfriend at a bar.

I went to the bathroom and into a stall. I pulled my pants down and sat on the toilet, hiding. The seat was heated and the warm felt nice. I gently lifted my nuts, slid forward, and put them down on the heated seat. I tried to relax. I smoked one on the toilet, hoping it would make me crap so I'd have a reason to be in this bathroom, but it only had 1 milligram of nicotine. I just wanted Camilla to tire herself out so we could go home.

When I got back to the bar, Camilla looked excited. She said, "Everyone's going to this club in a minute! Can we go with them?"

I said, "Do we have to?"

CHAPTER XXXIII

We walked down the street in Osaka around midnight, me and Camilla and ten Japanese people. I walked between Shogo and Camilla. She kept kissing me.

She whispered, in a saccharine way, "You're the sweetest, I'm so glad you're my boyfriend." She laughed. I felt paralyzed. The Japanese gangsters could tell we were lying.

I said, "Yeah, it's been great so far."

She said, "Why aren't you kissing me back?"

I said, "I don't know. I think the con is going well without it."

Camilla said, "You look stiff."

I said, "I feel like I'm in a play."

She whispered, "You know, if you were gay and I was pretending to be your girlfriend, this is exactly how you would look? Like you weren't enjoying it at all?"

We walked for a little while longer. I rubbed her back like an amputee at physical therapy getting used to a bionic arm.

Shogo looked at me and said, "Sleepy? You are? Go home?"

I tried to smile and said, "No, I'm good." I wanted to force a laugh but could only grimace.

I felt possessive of Camilla. I knew Shogo was trying to get me to go home so he could sleep with her. I felt insulted. I didn't know if Camilla was aware that Shogo was trying to sleep with her.

We stopped in front of a 7/11. Shogo pointed at the 7/11. He said, "Beer." He pointed to me and said, "Beer?"

I said, "Sure. Thank you." I took out $5 in yen and handed it to him. He refused to take it. I said, "Thank you," again.

He pointed to Camilla but looked only at me. He said, "She can have?"

Camilla said, "Yeah!"

Shogo ignored Camilla. He looked at me again. I must have looked confused.

He said, "For her? Beer? She can have?"

So he was asking me for permission to buy my apparent girlfriend beer. I guess, as the man, I controlled her.

I said, "Yeah, of course?"

He said again, "You are sleepy?"

I said, "No, no way, I'm fine."

Me, Camilla, and all of the girls stood outside as the men went into 7/11 to buy beer.

Camilla kissed me on the lips again. She said, "Thank you, daddy! For permission to drink."

I said, "It's even weirder when you call me daddy."

I put my hands on her shoulders and kissed her. It felt like my first kiss – I just wanted to get it over with. Her shoulders were strong.

They came back out and handed us beers. Camilla opened hers and drank a lot in one gulp. I couldn't open my can – the tab was too close to the top of the can. I fiddled with it and couldn't get my finger under the tab. I reached into my pocket for a coin to use for leverage.

Camilla took the can. She opened it and handed it back to me. Shogo saw it happen.

I said, "You're really fucking me here."

CHAPTER XXXIV

Outside the club, we met up with another group of Japanese skaters and their women. I stood with Shogo, Camilla, and the translator. Shogo said something to one of guys in Japanese and the guy got on his knees and bowed to me, over and over.

I said, "Oh, come on. You don't need to bow. Come on, get up." I reached out my hand to help him off the ground. He kept bowing.

He wouldn't stop. I must have been blushing. Camilla started kissing me again.

I said to the translator, "Why is he bowing to me?"

The translator said, "Shogo says, 'He goes on a trip to all Shpreme stores around the world.' Hayato love Shpreme also."

I said to the guy bowing, "Supreme! It's the best."

He stood up and smiled. He said, "Shpreme. Love."

CHAPTER XXXV

I sat by myself on a couch in the corner of the club. A strobe light went around.

Camilla danced with a group of girls dressed like Missy Elliott, in Adidas track suits and Kangol hats. Camilla almost kept up with them, but they looked like a professional dance troupe. It looked like one of the *Step Up* movies.

The way they danced reminded me of something the Airbnb host said on the way home – "If an American says they can do something, it means they've tried it once or twice. If a Japanese person says they can do something, it means they've advanced to the highest levels of the profession."

Camilla sat down next to me. She was out of breath from the dancing. She kissed me on the cheek again and I sat there with my eyes open, staring straight ahead.

She said, "Do you want me to stop?"

I said, "No, it's okay. It shores up the con."

She leaned in and kissed me on the lips. She slid her tongue into my mouth. I tried to remember how to do it.

I put out my tongue and lashed it around inside her mouth. It was not erotic. Camilla went back to the dancefloor.

Shogo came up to me. He pointed to himself and said, "Dancing? With C.?"

I looked down. I shrugged and said, "Knock yourself out."

Shogo and Camilla danced as I sat in the corner. I smoked

and sipped my beer furtively since I didn't buy it at this club. Sometimes I looked up and watched and they turned around and glanced at me, but mostly, they looked at each other. They got closer. The DJ played "Pony" by Ginuwine. I'm sure he would have played a more sexual song if one had ever been written. Camilla danced suggestively. No one respected me.

I finished the beer and felt extremely drunk. I thought about going up to a girl, but I couldn't dance and no one spoke English. I felt so alone. I wished I could call my mom. I wondered if I was going to pass out. I waited for the alcohol to fully enter my bloodstream because I'd read somewhere that it takes 40 minutes to reach peak drunkenness. I hoped I would pass out so Camilla would have to take me home.

Camilla came back and sat down next to me. A bead of sweat rolled down the side of her face.

Camilla said, "Shogo asked me if you were my boyfriend."

I said, "He didn't believe me that you were?"

I leaned in to kiss Camilla to assert my status as the man who controlled this woman. She turned her head and let me kiss her cheek.

Camilla said, "Maybe if you didn't look like you were stepping on a tack every time we kissed, he wouldn't have."

We sat there for a while longer. I stared at my lap.

Camilla said, "I told him you weren't gay."

I said, "What do you mean?"

Camilla looked puzzled.

I said, "Are you serious?! You didn't tell him I was your boyfriend?!"

Camilla nodded. She said, "What's the difference? I mean, he doesn't think you're gay. That's what you wanted, right? That's why we were acting like I was your girlfriend, right?"

I jumped up and grabbed my jacket and tried to put it on. I walked as fast as I could out of the club. I ran down the stairs, five flights, and walked out into the street. I just wanted to get away from this whole thing.

I tried to remember where I was. Somewhere in Japan, somewhere in Osaka, on a street outside a club in the middle of the night, five thousand miles from anyone I knew, with no money. I felt alone again. I lit one. How could I find my way home? Everything was in Japanese.

I stumbled down the street as fast as I could. I went into a 7/11 to get a rice triangle and be inside because it was cold. I wanted to figure out where I was and how to get back to the Airbnb.

Camilla burst through the 7/11 door. She came up to me as I was picking out a rice triangle. She was breathing heavily and looked so angry. Her jacket was only on one arm.

She screamed, "WHY DID YOU JUST FUCKING STORM OUT LIKE THAT? WHAT THE FUCK IS WRONG WITH YOU?"

I screamed, "I DIDN'T FUCKING FEEL SAFE, OBVIOUSLY?"

Camilla screamed, "YOU'RE SUCH A FUCKING PUSSY!"

I screamed, "I'M NOT A PUSSY! IT WAS REASONABLE! IT WAS BECAUSE YOU TOLD HIM I WASN'T YOUR BOYFRIEND! SO HE KNOWS I LIED TO HIM! AND CONSTRUCTED AN *ELABORATE* LIE! AND HE WAS OUR HOST! AND JAPAN HAS A CULTURE OF RESPECT! IT'S SO DISRESPECTFUL TO LIE TO YOUR HOST! HE BOUGHT US BEER! AND NOW HE KNOWS I LIED TO HIM! AND HE'S IN A FUCKING GANG! AND HE THINKS I AM GAY *AND* LIED TO HIM!"

She screamed something but I couldn't hear it because I was also screaming.

I continued screaming, "AND NOW THAT YOU LEFT, I COCK-BLOCKED HIM TOO! I CAN'T BELIEVE YOU JUST FUCKING DID THAT! WHY COULDN'T YOU JUST STICK TO THE CON? WE WERE IN THE FUCKING CON TOGETHER!"

The clerk stared at us from behind the register. There was no one else in the 7/11.

Camilla screamed, "WHY WOULD YOU LIE ABOUT SOME-THING DUMB LIKE THAT? YOU'RE SUCH A FUCKING IDIOT! YOU NEVER SHOULD HAVE EVEN SAID ANYTHING! AND PUT ME IN

THIS POSITION!"

I screamed, "YOU WERE THE ONE WHO OFFERED TO PRE-TEND TO BE MY FUCKING GIRLFRIEND! THAT WASN'T MY IDEA! I WANTED TO GO HOME!"

Camilla screamed, "IF YOU WEREN'T SO INSECURE ABOUT YOUR MANHOOD, I WOULDN'T HAVE HAD TO! AND YOU FUCK-ING LIKED IT!"

I said, quietly, in a way calculated to be as cutting as possi-ble, "I promise you, I've never been less into a sexual experi-ence than that."

Camilla looked hurt. She didn't say anything.

I said, "You couldn't conceive of me *not* being sexually attracted to you?"

And then she looked angry. She screamed, "YOU *MUST BE* FUCKING GAY! YOU HAVEN'T TALKED TO A GIRL ON THIS WHOLE FUCKING TRIP!"

I screamed, "BECAUSE WE WERE PRETENDING YOU WERE MY GIRLFRIEND!"

Camilla screamed, "AND BEFORE THAT?!"

I screamed, "NO ONE HERE SPEAKS FUCKING ENGLISH! I JUST WANTED TO GO FUCKING HOME AND WATCH *THE SIMPSONS* AND GO TO SLEEP! BUT YOU WANTED TO STAY AND FUCKING DANCE! YOU'RE SO FUCKING PRIMITIVE! JUST FLAILING YOUR FUCKING BODY AROUND? WHY WOULD I WANT TO FUCKING DO THAT? AND YOU DIDN'T EVEN NEED ME THERE ANYMORE! I JUST LOOKED PATHETIC! A CUCKOLD!"

I turned around and stumbled down the aisle as fast as I could. I stumbled out the front door and back onto the street and walked in any direction.

Camilla caught up to me. She said, "You have no idea where the fuck you're going, do you?"

I said, "I'm going *away* from you, you fucking crone."

She laughed at me. It made me upset.

Camilla counted these three points out on her fingers: "You have no money, you have no idea where you are, and I can't even believe you can walk right now from the pills alone, let alone everything you've had to drink."

I said, "How do you know what pills I've taken?"

I stumbled faster, trying to get away from her. After a block, she stopped walking and I kept going to I don't know where. Twenty feet further and I turned around and she was just standing there.

She was crying. Fuck her. I wanted to cry too. I was born alone and I would die alone.

She screamed, "AND YOU DON'T HAVE THE FUCKING AIRBNB KEY EITHER!"

I reached into my pocket. It wasn't there. She must have taken it out of my pocket.

She started walking in the other direction. I stood there. I thought about sleeping on the street again, but it was colder in Osaka than it was in Tokyo. I didn't want to do that again, but I didn't want to go back to her either. It felt like it would have been an admission that she'd won and that I needed her more than she needed me.

I watched her walk down the street, away from me. Thirty feet, fifty feet, the end of the next block, another block, and eventually, she was almost just a speck in my vision. I smoked the cigarette.

She won that one.

CHAPTER XXXVI

I caught up to her.

I ran up behind her and said, "Fuck you for stealing the key."

She said, through tears, "Don't talk to me, you fucking alcoholic drug addict freak. You ruined this trip before we even left."

I said, "No, fuck *you*."

Camilla said, "It would have been useless to you anyway – you would never have found your way home."

I said, "I would have."

She hiccupped.

For twenty minutes, we walked down the street in silence. I thought it was about 3:00 a.m. Nobody else was around. The only sounds were our feet, stumbling over the pavement.

I said, "Are you mad because I'm not into you? Sexually?"

She stopped walking.

When I realized, I stopped walking and walked back to her.

I said, "Come on, I'm fucking freezing."

CHAPTER XXXVII

We walked back the rest of the way to the Airbnb in silence. We walked up the stairs, through the entrance door, to the elevator, to the 8th floor, into the apartment, into the bedroom.

Camilla turned the light on. I turned it off.

I took off my jacket and my shoes and socks and my glasses. I grabbed my iPad and headphones out of my bag. I got into bed, as far as I could to one side until one of my butt cheeks was off the bed.

I turned over, facing the wall, facing away from her. I put on a *Simpsons* episode. I put my headphones on. I wished I was dead or had never come on this trip.

I checked iMessage on my iPad. No one had messaged me. I guessed it was late in New York too. And my friends were busy. A busy guy like myself associated with others who were busy, who had things going on.

I felt the mattress move. I knew Camilla had gotten into bed too.

I turned over to make sure she was as far away from me as possible.

Camilla sat up, on her knees, looking at me. She wasn't wearing a shirt.

We stared at each other for a second.

I said, "What are you doing?"

Camilla grabbed the cover and flung it away from me. She

climbed on top of me.

She leaned down close to my face. She looked me in the eye and said, "Are you still not into it?"

I tried to form some words. She seemed emotional. I was into it then.

We made out for a few minutes. It felt natural. I whispered, "I'm gonna have sex with you until you start crying, and then I'm gonna continue to have sex with you until you're fucking dead." I was just asking permission, but I also wanted her to feel like I had some power.

Camilla said, "No, you're not."

I said, "What do you mean? You don't want to?"

Camilla said, "We're gonna have sex, but I'm not gonna cry until afterwards."

While we had sex, I thought of this pearl of wisdom my camp counselor shared with the bunk when I was around 13: "The most important thing to remember in life is this: Sex isn't just masturbating into a woman."

And then, I said, "Are you only having sex with me because you were hurt that I wasn't into it when you were pretending to be my girlfriend? Like, to prove that I am sexually attracted to you?"

Camilla said, "Are you only having sex with me to prove to me that you're straight?"

I said, "I don't care if you think I'm gay."

After it was over, she said, "Did you fucking come inside me?"

I tried to collect myself. I said, sheepishly, "Not really? Maybe, like, 20%? I did the best I could."

She looked at me, half anger, half disbelief. She didn't say anything.

I didn't know what to say. I went to the bathroom. She lay on the bed, probably looking at the ceiling, although I couldn't see exactly what she was doing because I was in the bathroom.

I came back.

She said, "Please get the fuck out of this room."

I didn't want to argue with her this angry. I put my Flower Pants on. I got my iPad and my jacket. I walked out into the living room.

I curled up on the couch, shirtless in my jacket, and watched *The Simpsons* on my iPad on low volume so it wouldn't wake the Airbnb host. As a houseguest, my consideration was limitless. In the bedroom, I could hear her crying. She was right.

CHAPTER XXXVIII

I woke up hyperventilating in the middle of the night.

I reached into my pocket to take out an Ativan and a Mellow Yellow and chewed them both up. I found the bottle of whiskey in my jacket pocket and swished whiskey around in my mouth to get the little bits of pill in my teeth loose.

I lay there waiting for the panic to pass, trying to fall asleep. I couldn't fall asleep and the panic wouldn't pass, so I drank the rest of the whiskey. I went out onto the apartment's tiny balcony and smoked one.

I smoked four more and watched trucks go by on a raised highway. The highway was about 200 feet from the balcony, a few stories lower. I thought, "They're probably bringing fresh fish to 7/11." After I smoked the sixth one, I vomited over the side of the balcony. There was no one on the street.

CHAPTER XXXIX

In the morning, I knocked on the bedroom door and walked in. Camilla was using her phone with the Airbnb's Wi-Fi. She didn't look up at me.

I said, "Wanna go to the Osaka Aquarium today? Or Supreme?"

She didn't say anything.

I said, "The aquarium's supposed to be really sick. One of the world's biggest aquariums. Like, fish and stuff from every climate in the world. One second you're seeing, like, crabs from Ecuador, and then next to those are porpoises from Denmark. I read that in the guidebook."

She didn't say anything.

I said, "It's supposed to be really sick" again.

Camilla said, "I think I just want to be by myself today."

I said, "What are you gonna do?"

Camilla said, "Probably exactly what I'm doing now."

I said, "Being on your phone?"

She said, "Yes. Being on my phone."

I said, "But we're in Japan. Right? YOLO?"

She didn't look up.

She said, "I am going to YOLO. By myself. In bed. Sometimes, you can YOLO by being on your phone."

I said, "I thought being on your phone was the opposite of YOLOing."

Camilla said, "Have you ever tried to YOLO by shutting the fuck up, turning around, walking out of this room, and closing the door behind you?"

I said, "Do you know what 'YOLO' stands for?"

She didn't say anything.

I picked up my clothes. I turned around and walked out and closed the door behind me and got dressed in the living room.

I walked back into the bedroom.

I said, "Are you angry because you think I got you pregnant?"

Camilla pretended I wasn't there.

I said, "Because, like, the chance of getting pregnant is pretty small. 10% or something. And that's among people who are trying to get pregnant. A lot of couples try to get pregnant and can't. And I was already mostly through the process of, you know, like, 'vacating the premises' when it happened, too."

Camilla didn't say anything. I knew she wanted me to leave.

I said, "What are you doing on the phone?"

Camilla said, "Finding where to get Plan B. But it's fucking impossible because we're in fucking Japan."

I said, "You mean because of the population problem? They don't want people contraceiving?"

Camilla didn't look up at me or say anything.

I walked back out into the living room. I put on my shoes and jacket. I started walking towards the front door.

I turned around and walked back into the bedroom for the last time.

I said, "I don't think there's any chance you're pregnant. I've never gotten a woman pregnant. 'I don't even know if my boys can swim.'"

CHAPTER XL

I walked four miles through Osaka to the Osaka aquarium. I passed a baseball field of little Japanese kids in full baseball regalia, cleats and uniforms, practicing like a professional team. They all looked like baseball prodigies. The coaches directed them through the drills.

I stopped at a convenience store called Sunkus. The Airbnb host explained, on my walk with him, it was called Sunkus because that's how the English word "thanks" is pronounced by a Japanese speaker.

I got some more whiskey, fried chicken, and rice triangles. I ate them as I walked, wiping the grease on my pants.

I stopped at a tea vending machine and got a hot milk tea, but it was too sweet, like a melted milkshake. I threw it out.

I took a picture of a tall building with a blue top hat on top. At the ground floor entrance to the building, there was a sign that said, "Welcome to HI HAT AVE."

I stopped in front of a donut chain called Mister Donut. It had signs advertising the "Brooklyn Croissant Donut" and the "Brooklyn Jar," which was just a mason jar with a hole in the lid that you could put a straw into. The text next to the Brooklyn Jar on the sign said, "Use it as you like!"

I bought a Brooklyn Croissant Donut. It came in a special Brooklyn Croissant Donut bag. I said to the woman behind the counter, "I live in Brooklyn."

She didn't understand. I pointed to the part of the bag that said Brooklyn. I said, "Brooklyn" and pointed to myself.

She said, "Ah, Brooklyn! Cool. Where is?"

I said, "It's in New York City."

She said, "New York City! Cool. Super cool."

I logged onto the Mr. Donut Wi-Fi on my phone. I sent a picture of the Brooklyn Croissant Donut bag to a girl I'd slept with. She lived around the corner from the bakery where they invented the cronut. It was in Manhattan, not Brooklyn. She told me there was a line of tourists outside every morning. When she walked me to the subway, she looked at them and said, "Morons."

I sent a message that said, "I'm in Japan. They think the cronut is from Brooklyn. Little do they know!"

I sat there, eating the donut and waiting for her to text me back while I was still on the Wi-Fi. She didn't. She must have been busy.

I texted again, "This is David Shapiro btw", in case she didn't have my number anymore.

I walked past a gambling parlor called "Big Texas Gambling" and took a picture of a sign outside: "Texas is often taken out with an uncanny tip and is an excitement. It is air of a good flow."

Next to the aquarium, I rode the biggest Ferris wheel I'd ever been on. I tried not to look down. I looked up the Ferris wheel in the guidebook while I was riding it. It was the tallest Ferris wheel in the world from 1997 to 1999.

From the Ferris wheel, I could see Osaka Bay. I thought of the Cam'ron line where he said, "Hit you from a block away / Drinking sake on a Suzuki / We in Osaka Bay." I could also see some mountains but I couldn't identify them. Japan was full of mountains.

Outside the aquarium, a group of penguins stood in a pen on a floor of ice. They waddled around on the ice, lifting their heads up and spreading their wings. Putting their heads down and putting their wings back at their sides. The aquarium attendant next to the penguins talked to some little girls and their mother about the penguins in Japanese.

When she was done, I asked her if I could pet the penguins by pointing at the penguins and making a petting motion with a pleading look on my face. She made a gesture towards the penguins to tell me it was okay.

I pet a penguin on its head. It didn't move away from me. I pet it again. I wondered, "What does this thing think of me? I hope it doesn't bite me." I'd never had a pet. I pet it again and again. I liked this penguin. I didn't think it would bite me.

I felt a lump in my throat and kept petting the penguin. I thought I was going to cry soon, but I held back. I felt alone. The attendant told me to stop petting. I guess she thought the penguin had had enough. I didn't think so, but I had no way to communicate that.

The little girls looked at me. I thought, "I wonder what these little girls think of me? A stranger in a strange land, an American man who looks like he's about to cry, petting this poor penguin." Their mother took them away.

I browsed the gift shop in the aquarium. There was some funny English on some t-shirts. One had a cartoon of three cute sea otters, two of them standing behind a bigger one. The bigger one had a speech bubble coming out of its mouth that said "What's wrong?" The two little ones behind it had little speech bubbles coming out of their mouths that both said "What's?" I said it to myself in my head, "What's wrong? What's? What's?"

I bought an audio tour and got instructions on how to use it from an attendant. I'd always thought people at museums who got audio tours were losers because they were alone.

I walked down past the Aleutian Islands (rainbow trout) and Monterey Bay (seals and sea lions). I watched an otter-type thing swim back and forth, like it was doing laps. I walked past Panama Bay (a sloth), the Ecuadorian jungle (iguanas and a squirrel monkey), Antarctica (penguins), and the Tasmanian Sea (dolphins).

In front of the Pacific Ocean, the biggest tank in the aquarium, I started to cry. I couldn't control it. I cried like a little kid. I couldn't stop crying. I saw my reflection in the tank mirror and it didn't look like my face. I felt tears turn from warm to cool as they rolled down.

A whale shark, the largest fish species on Earth according to the audio tour, swam past me. I looked into one of its eyes. It couldn't cry because it was in the water, or if it could, no one would notice.

I sat on a bench near a bathroom and tried to keep my sobbing quiet. Families walked past me. The adults averted their eyes but the kids looked at me.

I coughed. It interrupted the crying. I thought, "Why am I even here? What the fuck am I doing? What am I supposed to do now?"

I wished I were home, in my bed. Or getting a green juice from Mr. Melon on Fulton and Washington. I wished there was one English-speaking person here I could talk to. I wished my phone worked and the girl I slept with would text me back. I wondered where she was.

I thought about jumping off the roof of the aquarium, but getting my body back to America would be so expensive for my parents.

I collected myself and walked down to the basement. I cried in front of some crustaceans and a jellyfish. I found a bathroom, walked into a stall, pulled my pants down, and sat down on the toilet. I punched myself on the thigh until I stopped crying.

I came out of the stall at the same time the guy in the stall next to me came out of his. He didn't even look at me. How could someone be so polite?

CHAPTER XLI

I wandered around the mall adjacent to the aquarium for three hours. I got drunk. I didn't want to go back to the Airbnb apartment. I imagined Camilla was patiently waiting there to ignore me completely.

I tried on clothes with funny English writing on them. I bought a hoodie that said "WE SHALL MEET EACH OTHER" and a hat that said "NO FUN!" And a long-sleeve t-shirt with a cartoon drawing of three pigs. Below the drawing, there was text that said, "Pig 3 Brothers: All my brothers are pigs, good friend good is carried out very much."

I walked home through Osaka at night. I stopped at a bakery and bought a mug with two wrapped cookies inside it for Camilla. It would be harder for her to ignore me if I came bearing gifts. The mug had a drawing of a dog and text that said, "The dog is a member of the family, so to speak." She would think that was funny.

And I'd apologize. It helped to apologize. It would put the emotional burden on her. Before I apologized, I'd done something wrong and hadn't taken responsibility. After I'd apologized, I guess I would still have done something wrong, but I'd have taken responsibility for it, so she would be the one obligated to get over it. I would have done all I could have. What more could I do than apologize?

I stopped at Burger King to try the BK Cheese Fondue. I

ordered it and walked upstairs and sat against the window, looking down at the people walking past on the street. Everyone else in the Burger King was alone too.

The waiter brought it to me – a bowl of hot cheese fondue and a burger. I dipped the burger in the thick cheese fondue. I ate a spoonful of fondue to see what it tasted like without the burger. It tasted like you'd expect.

I got home around 7:30. Camilla was gone. And her bags were gone. On the bed, there was a note that said, "I can't deal right now. I canceled all the Airbnb reservations except this one. Meet me in Fukuoka in 3 days. I'll email you about where we're staying when I know. Sorry."

CHAPTER XLII

I took the bullet train to Nagoya, forty minutes east of Osaka, to go to my fifth of six Japanese Supreme stores.

After riding on a train through Japan for hundreds of miles, I'd only seen maybe five or six people outside from the train window. The country felt empty. There were 130 million people in Japan. And it was smaller than California, and California had 40 million people – where were all the people?

From the train, none of the houses I saw were much bigger or much smaller than the others. No mansions. These people were all on the same team. I wished I were Japanese.

Nagoya was an industrial city. Dreary. I thought, "I wish, one time, a guidebook would just say, 'This place sucks, don't go here.'" I'd read online that Nagoya was one of the world's epicenters of metal music, but I didn't see any evidence of a metal scene as I walked down the street from the train station to Supreme at 2:30 in the afternoon.

I wished I were at home, laying on the couch in my living room, watching *The Simpsons*, watching the snow fall down outside my window.

I thought about my mom's face, a few weeks before I left for this trip, when she was crying in the car after she came to pick me up from my apartment at 4:45 a.m. My roommate had called her.

My roommate said, "Hi, Mrs. Shapiro?! David is vomiting!

He keeps vomiting. He's vomiting on my bed. I don't know what to do!"

My roommate was scared. Also angry that I'd vomited all over her bed. I'd lurched from my bedroom into her room and started vomiting onto her comforter. She was sleeping. I was just trying to get her attention.

She said, "What the fuck is wrong with you?! Get out of here! Go into the bathroom!"

I said, "I can't." I laid down on the floor.

My roommate said, "Are you drunk?"

I said, "No. I haven't had a drink in three days. That's the problem."

She said, "How is that a problem?"

I said, "I'm in alcohol withdrawal."

She said, "Do you need to go to the hospital?"

I said, "I don't know. You need to call my mom and ask her. She would know. Tell her I think I might have delirium tremens. Tell her not to tell my Dad."

When she got off the phone with my mom, I made her get me an Ativan from my backpack. I laid on the floor on my back and ordered her a new bed-in-a-bag on Amazon Prime with the one day shipping. $3.99 extra. It was worth it. She went into the living room and slept on the couch.

By the time my mom came to pick me up, I felt relaxed. Even, I guess, in a pretty good mood, relieved to not feel like I was about to die.

In the car on the way home, my mom cried so hard that she had to pull over. I rubbed her back. I said, "Mom, it's fine. Really. I feel much better now. I'm gonna be fine. Do you want me to drive?"

My mom put me to bed. I woke up fifteen hours later in my childhood twin bed. I needed one. I got one out of my backpack and smoked it in bed, ashing on the floor. I dropped the butt on the carpet and went back to sleep. My dad smelled it in the hallway. He came into my room. The noise from the door creaking open woke me up. He looked at me and stood there, shaking his head. I rolled over and faced the wall. My parents didn't know I smoked. I said, "I'm sorry." I couldn't watch him cry too. A whole crying family.

CHAPTER XLIII

The Nagoya Supreme store was small, tucked between two restaurants on the outskirts of the retail area of the city. The retail area had stores like Ralph Lauren and Gucci.

There were ghost sculptures hanging from the ceiling in the store. I tried to take pictures of them but the employees stopped me. I touched all of the clothes again, especially the fireman's coat and the Love Supreme tee. I loved the material, the heavy cotton.

They also had the Hardcore Hammer, from 2012. It was a hammer head mounted on an axe handle.

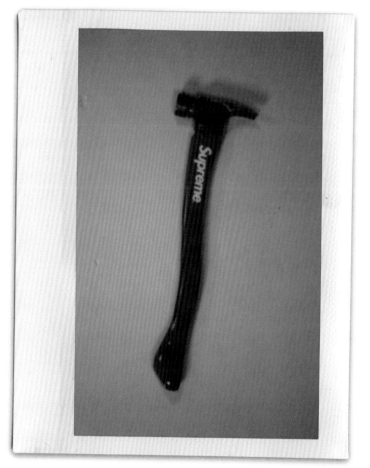

It cost about $100. I thought about buying it. I knew I had no use for a hammer, but I wanted to own it. I thought, "I could put it on the bookshelf in my apartment next to the other accessories. Maybe I could sell it on eBay in five years. I could make good use of this hammer."

But I recognized that buying this hammer was not dissimilar to just lighting my money on fire. So I promised myself that I wouldn't buy the hammer here, but if they had it in Fukuoka, I would buy it there. I could only resist for so long. I was only a man.

CHAPTER XLIV

I sat on a bench in the middle of the store for two hours. I listened to music on my headphones and looked around. I missed Camilla. No other customers came in. I had the place to myself and the employees didn't say anything to me.

Supreme was like a movie in another language without subtitles. On the rack hung a jacket that looked like a Helmut Lang jacket. I found out about this on a men's fashion forum:

From reading Wikipedia and reading Supreme forums, I knew Helmut Lang was a prominent New York fashion designer in the 1990s. In 2005, he stopped calling himself a fashion designer and started calling himself an artist. In 2010, he shredded his archive of clothes and turned the shreds into sculptures. And then Supreme made that jacket. But I didn't understand what it meant. I should have studied art in college.

I walked to Ralph Lauren and took some clothes into the dressing room, but they were too small for me. Japanese sizes.

I bought rice triangles and Doritos (creamed corn soup flavor) from 7/11 and walked to the Ferris wheel in the center of the city. I rode it twice, eating the Doritos and wiping the flavor dust on my pants.

I walked to the Toyota Museum that I saw in the guide-book. I bought a ticket. I looked through a museum map and realized that although I thought the museum was going to be all about Toyota cars, according to the map, the museum was all about textiles. That's how Toyota started.

I walked through the museum, touching the fabrics they'd made, mostly cotton.

I walked through acres of looms, big machines that took raw cotton and wrapped it together and out popped cotton fabric. Looms from the 1890s, bigger looms from the 1920s, spinning looms used to make the cottons that outfitted Japanese soldiers during World War II, the entire modern evolution of the loom. It was boring. I didn't give a shit about looms.

I got a room at a Ryokan, a traditional Japanese inn, that I'd found in the guidebook. It was about 20 minutes away from Supreme. I ordered a traditional Japanese breakfast for the next morning by checking a box on the hotel room contract.

I bought a beer from a beer vending machine in the lobby and put my bags in my room. I grabbed my iPhone and my Jambox. I took an Ativan and enough Mellow Yellow to kill a person whose body wasn't acclimated. I walked out the back door of the Ryokan, through a little garden, towards the traditional Japanese bath. It was housed in a separate building.

I took my clothes off and washed myself in a separate room before walking into the room with the bath, as the instructions on the wall told me to do.

CHAPTER XLV

There was no one else at the traditional Japanese bath. It was like a Jacuzzi, but square and sunken into the ground. It could fit fifteen people. The water was warm. Steam rose out of it, not because the water was that hot, but because the air was cold.

I sat naked in the hot bath with the water up to my chest. I watched the steam rise and listened to music on a low volume out of my Jambox.

I felt peaceful but still alone. There was nothing I could do about it. I drank the beer. I peed in the pool and pushed the pee water away from me. I played with my dick, pointing it up towards me and looking at its eye. I looked at it and thought, "Why do you fuck with me, dick?"

I woke up at around 7:00 a.m. in the bath. My hands were wrinkly and I was thirsty. The Jambox battery was dead. I went back to my room, took a shower, and ate my traditional Japanese breakfast alone in the Ryokan's ballroom.

Breakfast was served on little dishes: a little plate with one slice of kiwi and one slice of grapefruit, a little bowl with a few leaves of lettuce and some carrot, a bowl with miso soup, a bowl of rice. A small segmented tray with a raw quail egg in one segment and pieces of raw fish and radish in the other. Another small plate with just pieces of raw fish.

A bowl with a small rock on fire inside it cooked a chicken

egg suspended above the rock in what looked like a coffee filter. I thought, "What a neat contraption," but I worried the rock was going to overcook the egg. I hoped the waiter would come back to blow the rock out before the egg burned, but he never came back.

The rock's flame went out when the egg was perfectly cooked. I realized it was designed for this purpose, with just enough fuel to cook the egg.

I ate the food and thought, "This dainty food is never going to fill me up. I need fried chicken."

CHAPTER XLVI

I took the bullet train to Hiroshima, two hundred and ninety-eight miles west. There was no Supreme store there but I was curious about the bombing. And I had time. And my rail pass was unlimited.

I saw three American couples on the train, more white faces than I'd seen together since the airport in Tokyo. They must also have been curious about the destruction we'd wrought in Hiroshima.

After looking at only Japanese people for so long, the faces of the white people looked disgusting. I thought, "Are these ugly white people or have I just adjusted to Japanese faces as normal?"

I looked them over more closely as we took the escalator down to the street. I thought, "No, these white people are definitely decent looking. It's me."

I got a room at the Sheraton Hiroshima next to the train station. It had a Western-style bed so I didn't have to sleep on the floor. I connected to the hotel Wi-Fi and tried to Face-Time my friends in New York, but it was 5:00 a.m. there. No one answered.

I walked through Hiroshima, a valley of skyscrapers. I looked around for hints of destruction, like memorials, wreaths laid against sculptures, big statues, but there were none.

I walked over a bridge. I walked through a covered, arcade-style mall. I looked at some hoodies with writing across the chest. One said "COFFEE & MUFFIN" and another said "TODAY." Another said, "UP TO YOU."

At the Hiroshima Peace Memorial Museum, I paid about 50 cents in yen to get in.

In the first room, there was a scene of mannequins walking through the city in the minutes after the bomb went off. In the background, the city was on fire. They walked through rubble, burned all over, tattered clothes hanging off their bodies.

Personal artifacts recovered from the scene were in glass cases around the room: a melted watch, a pair of melted eyeglasses, a melted tricycle.

In the center of the room was a model of the city with a red ball hanging above it, the atomic bomb fireball about a second after it exploded, 2000 feet over the ground.

I wanted to walk up to a Japanese person and apologize, but it would have been so stupid.

In another room, there was a staircase taken from the front of a bank building where someone was sitting, waiting for the bank to open, when the bomb went off. There was a dark shadow where they were sitting, where their body blocked the heat from the blast.

I left the Peace Museum. I found a 7/11, bought a potato sandwich and some more creamed corn soup flavored Doritos, and walked to the river that ran through the city.

I sat on the side of the river, eating the potato sandwich and the Doritos. They were shaped like Christmas trees and did taste like creamed corn soup. In the Peace Museum, I'd read that thousands of corpses floated down this river after the blast because people jumped into the river to relieve the pain from the atomic bomb burns, but they didn't survive. That I was sitting there, eating the creamed corn Doritos and thinking about the corpses, it didn't mean anything, but I wanted to mention it.

CHAPTER XLVII

When I got back to the hotel room, Camilla had emailed me the address and check-in time for the Airbnb in Fukuoka. I wrote back, "Sweet. I will be there. I am in Hiroshima if you happen to be here too and decide you want to reconvene with me early."

I took a nap. When I woke up, I checked my email. She hadn't written back.

It was morning in New York.

I FaceTimed my ex-girlfriend, who I dated for three years but then only saw when I bumped into her at the deli. We went to the same deli because we lived around the corner from each other.

It rang for a long time. I laid on the bed and thought, "I am prepared to keep calling until she picks up or her phone dies."

She answered. I saw her pixelated face on the screen. She was wearing headphones.

She looked confused.

I said, "Hi, Kat."

She whispered, "Why are you FaceTiming me?"

I said, "I just wanted to talk."

She whispered, "I'm at *work*."

She lifted the phone over her head to show me that she was at work. People were working quietly on computers at long rows of desks behind her. She worked at *Vox* or *Mic* or something.

I pleaded, "Can we talk? I haven't talked to anyone in a long time. Days. I'm by myself."

She looked annoyed. She whispered, "I'm at work."

I said, "Could you go into a conference room?"

She looked around and thought about this for a second.

She whispered, "Fine. But I can only talk for five minutes."

I said, "That's all I need. Five minutes of human contact."

She whispered, "This isn't human contact."

I said, "It's close enough."

She put her phone into her pocket and walked into a conference room. I could hear her walking.

She took it out and looked at me on the screen.

She said, in an annoyed voice, "What do you need, David?"

I said, "Can you look at the camera lens when you're talking and at the screen while I'm talking? Just to make it feel like eye contact, at least when the other person's talking. And I'll do the same. Otherwise, we both look like we're looking down."

She sighed. She said, "Sure, whatever." She looked into the lens.

I said, "I wish they could put a lens right in the middle of the screen so it would feel like actual eye contact when you videochatted."

She said, "Are you calling just to annoy me? Or do you need something?"

I said, "How are you?"

She said, "I'm fine."

I said, "How's your new boyfriend?"

She said, "Is that why you're calling?"

I said, "No, I'm just curious."

She said, "He's great."

I said, "That's good."

Neither of us said anything for a second. Then she looked

at me on her screen with something like sympathy. I love sympathy. I guess I looked fucked up.

She said, "Are you in bed? That doesn't look like your bed."

I said, "I'm in Japan. In Hiroshima. In a hotel."

She said, "Why?"

I said, "Going around the world to every Supreme store."

She said, "Is Hiroshima spooky? I've always wanted to go there."

I said, "You're not surprised that I'm going around the world to every Supreme store? I thought you would at least be like, 'David, you're so crazy!'"

She said, "I already know you. If you want someone to react like that, call someone you didn't spend three years with."

I said, "I see what you're saying."

She said, "So is Hiroshima spooky?"

I said, "Not at all. They rebuilt the whole city in like 13 years. Faster than the Freedom Tower."

She said, "Is there a Supreme store there?"

I said, "No, I just wanted to see what Hiroshima was like. I had a free few days."

She said, "Free from what?"

I said, "Camilla."

She said, "What do you mean?"

I said, "We had sex and then she wanted to get away from me."

Neither of us said anything for a few seconds.

She said, "What's it like?"

I said, "I'm used to it."

She said, "No – I meant, what's Hiroshima like?"

I said, "Just feels like a normal Japanese city."

She said, "I've never been to Japan – I don't know what a normal Japanese city is like."

I said, "It's quiet, extremely clean, everyone's fastidiously polite. Huge buildings. Tiny cars. Basically crime-free. And all the people are Japanese."

She said, "I see."

I said, "Can I tell you a funny story? Or, like, a story. I don't know if it's funny. But you might get a kick out of it."

She said, "If it'll take less than four minutes."

I said, "Do you remember the Supreme ashtray you bought me for my birthday like two years ago?"

She said, "The red one? That rips off the Hermes ashtray designs, according to you?"

I said, "Yeah."

She said, "What about it?"

I said, "Do you remember, like a year after you bought it for me, when I found out it was selling for like $300 on eBay?"

She said, "And you asked me if you could sell it on eBay even though I'd given it to you for your birthday? How could I not remember?"

I said, "Well, so, anyway, after you broke up with me, when I was angry, the first thing I did was sell it on eBay."

She laughed. She said, "I understand that. How much did you get for it?"

I said, "$325."

She said, "Wow."

I said, "But it cracked during shipping. And when the buyer got it, this kid in California, he started sending me these crazy eBay messages, really livid, demanding a refund and saying that he was going to report me to eBay. I think he thought I sold him one that was already cracked and I would argue to eBay that he cracked it. So I could keep his money."

She said, "What'd you do?"

I said, "I just issued him the refund through PayPal with a request for him to send it back to me. And then the next day, he wrote back saying that he was going to overnight it back to me, and the shipping would be $70, and I should PayPal it to him immediately."

She said, "Did you?"

I said, "Fuck no. I emailed him back and wrote, like, '$70? Come on. I would literally rather you send me a video of you smashing it with a baseball bat in a parking lot than make me pay $70 to send it back.'"

She laughed again. She said, "Did he offer to ship it back in a cheaper way?"

I said, "He sent me a video of him smashing it with a baseball bat in a parking lot."

She laughed for a long time. I laughed too.

I said, "He put it on YouTube. It has like a hundred-something-thousand views. Maybe almost 200,000 views. It was big on Supreme message boards. I can send you the link."

She said, "Did you leave him bad feedback?"

I said, "I couldn't, or he would leave me bad feedback. I need to keep my feedback 100% or it hurts my selling listings in eBay's search algorithm. I didn't leave him any feedback at all. I just wrote him back, like, 'F you, dude. Just, like, f you. Go f yourself. I hope you sit on an f'ing nail. I hope your parents walk in front of a bus.' Stuff like that. Couldn't say 'fuck' or eBay wouldn't let the message go through. And then a couple of days later, he sent me $70 on PayPal. Maybe he felt bad. Or made some money off YouTube ads."

Kat smiled.

I said, "And he also collected the shards and sent them back to me in a box. The shipping was like $2.38, fucking Media Mail. And then he left me 5-star feedback."

She said, "Did you take the opportunity to give him negative feedback, knowing he couldn't take his back?"

I said, "No. I gave him 5 stars too. He earned it. And then I got some gorilla glue and put the ashtray back together. It looks totally fucked up now, but you can still use it as an ashtray. I didn't even use it as an ashtray before. I didn't want to damage it. But now, I don't feel bad using it as an ashtray because it's, not, like, an objet d'art anymore. Although I am a little concerned about resting the burning tip of a cigarette in glue because, like, inhaling the burnt glue could be carcinogenic."

She said, "You know cigarettes are themselves carcinogenic, right?"

I nodded. I said, "Different kinds of cancer. Trying to manage my risk."

I looked at her on FaceTime for a second.

I said, "I miss you. I thought the story was, like, a metaphor for our relationship somehow, but I'm not exactly sure how. The ashtray is like a boomerang cursed by our relationship. I sent it away and it came back to me destroyed."

She said, "Don't say anything like that. If you say something like that again, I'm hanging up and going back to work."

I said, "I didn't mean sexually. I just meant, like, your company. You as a person in my life."

She just looked at the screen.

I said, "When I come back, do you wanna come over, have a drink, smoke some cigarettes and use the ashtray?"

She shook her head.

I said, "Why not?"

She said, "I don't think my boyfriend would like that."

I said, "He can come too."

She said, "I think he would rather have a growth removed from his neck than have a drink with you."

I said, "Does he have growths on his neck?"

We looked at each other again.

She said, "I have to go back to work now."

I said, "Thanks for talking to me."

She shrugged and said, "Good luck with the trip."

I took the elevator down to the hotel bar. I took a seat at the bar and looked at the menu. I looked around for other Westerners but there were none. And the drinks were like $20.

I walked back to the elevator, went up to my room, and chewed up some Mellow Yellow. I took the elevator back downstairs. I went into the workout room. I did the elliptical for five minutes before I got too winded to keep going.

I took the elevator back up to my room. I turned on the bath, got the temperature just right, put music on on my Jambox, Fucked Up, "Queen of Hearts." I put the Jambox on the floor next to the tub, drank five ounces of vodka, took my clothes off, looked at my weird body in the mirror, and got into the bath. "Hello, my name is David! Your name is Veronica!" Those are some lyrics. I screamed along. I got out of the bath to get the vodka and got back in. "The boot off my throat! Life is returning! Let's all emote!" I fell asleep with the water running.

CHAPTER XLVIII

In the morning, the bathroom was flooded and the carpet outside was soaking wet. I dropped my room key off in a slot in the lobby. Express Checkout.

I took my last bullet train to Fukuoka, "the Portland of Japan" according to the guidebook. One hundred and fifty-nine miles west on a separate island.

I took a cab to the Airbnb. I entered the door code provided in Camilla's email and walked into the apartment. It was small and full of trinkets and toy figurines.

I said, "Hi? Are you here?"

I felt so nervous.

I heard Camilla say, "Yeah, I'm here, in the bedroom." She sounded nervous too.

I walked back through the apartment and came to the bedroom door. Camilla was on a sleeping mat, using her laptop. I didn't want to have to sleep on the floor again, but I wouldn't say anything.

I said, "Hi."

She said, "Hi."

I put my bags down.

I said, "How are you?"

She said, "I'm better."

I said, "Are you still angry?"

She said, "I'm over it."

I walked over to her and sat down next to her. Not too close.

I said, "What'd you do on your days off from babysitting me?"

She said, "Went to Kyoto."

I said, "Are you sure you're not still mad?"

She said, "Yeah."

I said, "How was Kyoto? Did you see the temples?"

She said, "It was cool, but all these cities are starting to feel the same. I saw some temples. Those were all pretty much the same too."

I said, "Are white peoples' faces starting to look disgusting to you?"

Camilla said, "Yes! Oh my god. I thought it was just me."

We both laughed. I guess she was over it, maybe.

She said, "I actually, weirdly, like, missed going to Supreme. I feel like I haven't been to a Supreme store in ages, even though it's only been like four days."

I said, "I feel the same way."

Camilla said, "Did you go to the Nagoya one?"

I said, "Of course. But that feels like a long time ago also."

Camilla said, "How was it?"

I said, "To you, same as all the other ones. Same wallpaper and everything. To me, palace of the mind."

Camilla said, "Did they have any random old stuff?"

I said, "Yeah, the Hardcore Hammer."

I showed her the Hardcore Hammer on eBay. $188.88 Buy It Now.

She said, "How much was it at the store?"

I said, "About $100. I didn't buy it. It seemed super stupid. I don't use hammers. But it does go along with my theory of their accessories being underworld-connoted. An everyday household tool that movie gangsters use to smash fingers."

Camilla said, "Couldn't you tie just about any household item to either drugs or violence?"

I shrugged. Maybe she was right.

Camilla said, "What was Nagoya like otherwise?"

I said, "Sucked. I'm tired of Japan. I think Japan is the most boring place on earth."

Camilla said, "Don't be ignorant. Japan's amazing."

I said, "Japan is like *Pleasantville*. No public disorder. Not even music playing in a car. None of those black spots of gum on the pavement. No, like, street life. You know? Like, what happens here? What's on the front page of the newspaper? 'Cat stuck in tree'?"

Camilla said, "Earthquakes, nuclear disasters, stuff like that."

I said, "But that's not, like, the day-to-day. I'm talking about, like, walking down the street. I never thought I'd miss getting asked for money on the street outside my apartment. Or hearing people screaming at each other on the street. But then I came to Japan. It feels, like, dead. Except this one guy in Tokyo. But I've passed thousands of people since him."

Camilla said, "Why do you call that boring rather than, like, perfect? Or, like, this culture has figured out a way of living that's more frictionless than ours?"

I said, "I can feel two ways about it. I can contain multitudes. I've definitely thought, like, 'This is the most civilized place on earth.' But, like, for example, in every place we've been in that sells sandwiches, they have the crusts already cut off. Have you noticed that?"

Camilla said, "So?"

I said, "Everywhere in this country, every sandwich has the crust cut off. Doesn't that strike you as almost self-parodic? Like, 'Mussolini kept the trains running on time.' Whoever is in charge here keeps the trains running on time *and* the crusts cut off all the sandwiches."

Camilla said, "You're just wrong about it being 'boring.' Boring is the wrong word."

I said, "It can be both boring and perfect. Like a Toyota Camry."

Camilla said, "But when you lead with boring, you're misrepresenting it."

I said, "It's not like I'm giving a talk at the U.N. It's just you and me here."

CHAPTER XLIX

We walked to the Fukuoka store in the rain. We passed a Geisha using an iPhone.

I said, "I didn't know there were still Geishas? Just, like, walking around?"

Camilla said, "I didn't know they used iPhones."

I drank some whiskey from a bottle in my backpack.

Camilla said, "You smell like a distillery."

I said, "Is that bad?"

Camilla said, "It's not great."

I reached into my backpack and took out a dryer sheet from a little box I brought. I put it into my back pocket.

Camilla said, "What the fuck is that?"

I said, "A dryer sheet. Someone told me that if you put one in your back pocket, it makes you smell good all day. Like your clothes are freshly laundered. I've found that it works."

We walked, sharing an umbrella.

Camilla said, "I'm having a really good hair day today. There's no girl around to tell that to, but I wanted to get it out."

I said, "That's great."

Camilla said, "And I really like my outfit."

I said, "It's a cool outfit."

I got a sausage on a stick at 7/11. We went back out into the rain.

I said, "Can I ask you a question? Now that you seem to be in a good mood and don't appear to want me to perish from the earth."

Camilla said, "Go for it."

I said, "Can we sleep together again? I feel like I didn't get a chance to show my stuff. Like, it was a poor performance. I feel like, if given another opportunity, I could 'rock the Casbah' as they say."

Camilla said, coquettishly, "You mean you don't want to do it just to make love to me?"

I said, "Well, that could be part of it obviously."

Camilla laughed. She said, "I don't want to see your dick again for the rest of my life."

I said, "What if you just don't look at it? Like, close your eyes. Or I could wear boxers and put it through the hole."

Camilla ignored my suggestion.

She said, "Did you know 'Rock the Casbah' has nothing to do with sex? It's about political repression."

I said, "The song? The Clash song?"

Camilla said, "Yeah."

I said, "I didn't know that. How do you know that?"

Camilla said, "Don't worry about it."

I said, "I hate when people say that."

She said, "I know. Everyone does. That's why I said it."

CHAPTER L

At the Fukuoka store, I touched all the clothes. Camilla waited outside. I bought the Hardcore Hammer and I loved it.

I walked outside and we stood under an awning, not wanting to go back out into the rain. My shoes were full of water.

I said, "I bought the hammer."

Camilla said, "I thought you said it was stupid?"

I said, "I promised myself I wouldn't buy it in Nagoya on the condition that if they had it at Fukuoka, I would buy it here. That was the only way I could avoid buying it there."

Camilla said, "Why would you just… Not buy it at all?"

I said, "I couldn't help myself. I hate this company for tricking me into buying all this useless crap. But I can't stop."

Camilla said, "You don't have much discipline, do you?"

I said, "I do in other areas of my life. Like, not masturbating. You think that's easy?"

Camilla said, "I don't masturbate. I wouldn't call it a struggle exactly."

I said, "It's different for women."

Camilla said, "I knew you would say that. All men think that. But how do you know?"

I said, "Men and women want different things out of sex. Like, men want to impregnate lots of women, moving from town to town and whatnot. I don't know what women want exactly, but I know women like to cuddle after sex. I just want to just watch *The Simpsons*."

Camilla said, "Did you want to watch *The Simpsons* after we had sex?"

I said, "I did. I did watch *The Simpsons* after we had sex."

We walked for a long time in the rain. The bottoms of my pant legs became soaked.

Camilla said, "You're really lost."

I said, "What do you mean?"

Camilla said, "Like, intellectually *lost*. You have no idea what you're talking about or doing."

We spent three more rainy days in Fukuoka. I slept on the couch, the bathroom floor, and then the couch again.

CHAPTER LI

We flew to Seoul and wandered around the airport, waiting for the flight to London. I bought cigarettes for $19 a carton. I said to Camilla, "They're practically paying me to smoke these."

We walked past a bakery in the airport and Camilla looked at a scone. She said, "Does that look good?"

I said, "No, it's a scone."

Camilla said, "Scones can be good?"

I said, "They can't."

We shared one in a designated smoking area on a terrace at the airport. Camilla took it from me.

She took a drag. She said, "Ew. The tip is warm. And you slobbered on it."

She handed it back to me.

I said, "Can I coin a term?"

Camilla said, "No."

I said, "It's 'Bushwick Banquet.' Like, when you go to the deli and get like six bags of chips and eat them instead of a meal."

Camilla said, "What's that from?"

I said, "What do you mean?"

Camilla said, "Is that from a movie or something? Or, like, *Broad City?*"

I said, "No? It's from my mind, where I come up with all of

the things I think and say."
Camilla thought for a second.
She said, "I don't like it. Poor, minority neighborhood. Skipping meals in favor of junk food. *You* saying it... Just smells offensive."
I said, "You're right. But I didn't mean it that way."

CHAPTER LII

We flew to London, twelve hours. On the plane, I took some Mellow Yellows and put on *Godzilla* again. I waited to pass out.

Camilla came back from the bathroom. Something was wrong.

I said, "Is everything okay with you?"

Camilla said, "I just feel weird. I'm homesick."

I said, "Me too."

Camilla said, "You probably have some industrial strength sleeping pills on you, don't you?"

I said, "Yeah, but I wouldn't take a sleeping pill now, because if you wake up, like from turbulence or something, you'd probably hallucinate and maybe freak out. You should take a Mellow Yellow instead."

She said, "All right, Dr. Dave."

I gave her one.

She said, "Do you take this every day?"

I said, "Among other things. It's a muscle relaxant."

She said, "How's it going to make me feel?"

I said, "It'll knock you out. And when you wake up, you'll feel emotional. I don't know why. This is the one that makes people cry. That's why it's not that popular – they've developed muscle relaxants that don't make people cry."

Camilla took it.

I said, "Aside from feeling homesick, I also feel peaceful. I think, if I died right now, I would be okay with it."

Camilla said, "Yeah, I would be okay with that too."

I said, "Zing! You zinged me. You brought some real zingers on this trip."

She half-smiled.

I said, "Also, I take the dying thing back. It sounds corny."

She watched the new *Teenage Mutant Ninja Turtles*, waiting for the pill to kick in.

She turned it off. She reached over to my head and pulled my headphones down around my neck.

She said, "Can I tell you something?"

I said, "No," and put my headphones back on.

She pulled them down again and whispered, "Seriously."

I said, "Okay, what?"

She said, "My boobs are big."

I thought about this for a second. I said, "I know."

She whispered, "No, they're really big."

I said, "I am aware."

She whispered, "Like, bigger than they ever have been. And they hurt."

I said, "Do you want Tylenol?"

Camilla said, "Are you understanding what I'm saying?"

I said, "Is there a hidden message in the statement, 'My boobs are big'?"

Camilla said, "It means I think I'm pregnant. Are you fucking retarded?"

CHAPTER LIII

In London, we stayed with Camilla's sister in a house south of the river, in Battersea. Camilla didn't talk to me much. She made me pay for the taxi from the airport to the house. So expensive. Everything in London cost the same in pounds as it did in New York in dollars, but pounds were worth 1.5 times as much as dollars.

We got to the house at night. We put our bags down in the guest rooms.

I walked to a small supermarket called Tesco and asked for pregnancy tests, but they didn't sell them. I found a pharmacy and got two pregnancy tests in case one was defective.

I came back to the house. We went upstairs while Camilla's sister talked on the phone in the kitchen downstairs. I could hear the sound of her voice, but not the words, as I stood outside the bathroom.

Camilla went into the bathroom and peed on one. She brought it out of the bathroom. We sat on the bed in the guest room and waited for something to happen with the pregnancy test. It smelled like pee.

And then only the line appeared, no cross. I read the back of the box. She wasn't pregnant. What a relief.

She said, "I want to try the other one. I need to make sure."

I said, "Smoke 'em if you got 'em."

She peed on the other one and came back and sat down on

the bed next to me. Same thing. Not pregnant.

I said, "Should we celebrate?"

Camilla didn't say anything for a long time.

And then she said, "Why don't you take some pills and pass out?"

CHAPTER LIV

The next day, I walked through London to Supreme and Camilla stayed at home with her sister. Her sister didn't like me. I guess she'd told her sister I'd gotten her pregnant and she didn't even really want to sleep with me in the first place. And then, when she'd found out she wasn't pregnant, her sister still didn't like me. I could understand that.

As I left, Camilla and her sister sat on the couch in the living room, steeping bags of tea and watching *Friends.* Camilla half-heartedly asked me if I wanted to watch. I didn't even want to look at the TV.

I said, "Did you know that Supreme and *Friends* started in the same year?"

Camilla said, "Does *Friends* make you miss the old New York?"

I said, "It makes me hate the new New York."

I bet, if Supreme was a person instead of a brand, it would also hate *Friends.* It probably wouldn't like me, but it would definitely hate *Friends.* At least I do drugs. A little edge.

Her sister asked me, half-heartedly, what I thought of Japan.

I said, "It was less expensive than I thought it was going to be. Pretty reasonable, actually."

Camilla said, "That's because you ate all of your meals at 7/11."

CHAPTER LV

On the walk, I noticed that London had garbage in the street. And the people who worked at the convenience stores weren't nice.

I thought, "It makes sense why these people are on our team when we have world wars. The people who have rock and roll are on one team. And garbage in the street. The people who make the trains run on time are on the other." I had no one to share this insight with.

I walked past Big Ben, Westminster Abbey, the big Ferris wheel on the Thames, Buckingham Palace. Somewhere around here, they signed the Magna Carta, half the city was destroyed in World War II, world history was made for like a thousand years. I didn't give a shit about that, I just wanted to sit in Supreme.

CHAPTER LVI

Supreme London was the only Supreme store with two floors. I came in and walked downstairs and touched all of the Fall/Winter 2014 season clothes for the last time. When I got back to New York, the Spring/Summer 2015 season would be out.

On one of the walls of the London Supreme store, there was a collection of Supreme skateboard decks – the ones designed by Damien Hirst, Nate Lowman, etc. I stood there for a long time, admiring their designs and thinking about how much they would sell for on eBay. The Gagosian Gallery in New York sold the Nate Lowman ones for $5,000.

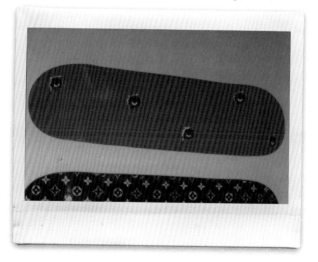

The Damien Hirst one had dots on it. Different colors. Evenly spaced. There didn't seem to be any pattern to the colors of the dots. I wished I could go up to one of the employees and say, "Can you explain this to me?"

I walked back upstairs and looked at the accessories in the display case. There was an employee behind the counter who looked at me but didn't say anything. I bought two packs of Supreme Post-It notes to justify my presence on the bench outside the store.

And then Jason Dill, a professional skateboarder who'd been the face of Supreme since the company started, walked in. He had a thick mustache and was wearing black suit pants, black and white shoes, and a Supreme jacket and shirt. And a pair of clear plastic sunglasses.

I texted Camilla, "Holy shit Jason Dill is here".

She didn't reply.

I texted again, "He's been the face of Supreme since it started. He's a famous skateboarder".

She didn't reply.

I texted again, "This is like going on a trip to Vatican City and seeing the Pope walking around".

Camilla texted back, "Take a picture".

Jason Dill talked to the employee behind the counter. The employee got him a bag of clothes from the back room.

I sat on the bench outside and tried to listen to their conversation, but I couldn't hear it over the music playing.

Jason Dill came out and sat down on the bench next to me. He looked through the clothing in the bag. I stared straight ahead, trying not to seem like I noticed him. He rifled through his bag and then looked out at the street. I wondered if he was going to leave. I was going to miss my chance.

I turned to him.

I said, "Hi, are you Jason?"

He looked at me. He looked me over. He said, "Yeah?"

I reached out my hand and said, "I'm David. It's an honor

to meet you. And a privilege. An honor and a privilege."

He shook my hand. He said, "Nice to meet you too."

I said, "I'm on a trip to every Supreme store in the world."

He said, "Why?"

I said, "I just love it. I don't know. I'm trying to understand it."

He laughed.

He said, "That's commendable. If anyone says it's lame, tell them to go fuck themselves."

I said, "Okay, I will. And now, I can tell them Jason Dill said I should tell them to go fuck themselves."

He said, "If you go to Osaka, and one of the other ones in Japan, the far one, you've got me beat."

I said, "Fukuoka?"

He said, "Yeah. Those are the ones I haven't been to."

I said, "I already went to those. They were cool."

He said, "They send me to Japan, like, four times a year."

I said, "Supreme?"

He said, "Yeah."

I said, "Do you like Japan?"

He said, "I mean, I like it. But four times a year? I like steak too, and I don't want to eat it every fucking night. But they put me up in a nice hotel in Shibuya, so it's cool."

I said, "Shibuya was nice."

I couldn't think of anything to say after that.

He said, "Where do you live?"

I said, "I live in New York. But I'm not really welcome in the store there. I wrote a magazine story about it that I think they didn't like. I mean, it was online-only, but it was for a magazine."

He looked at me curiously.

I said, "It was about the store in Chinatown that resells Supreme stuff? On *The New Yorker* website?"

He said, "Oh, shit, I think I read that?" He sounded surprised.

I said, "Ah, cool. I hope you liked it."

He nodded. I didn't know what this meant.

I said, "Do you live in London?"

He said, "No, I'm just here for work."

I said, "For Supreme?"

He nodded.

I said, "Can you tell me about your relationship with Supreme?"

He laughed. He said, "James is my boss. He took me in when I was 16. I just walked into the store, the first day it was open, and hung out there. And then never left. I owe him a huge debt."

I said, "I guess I do too."

We talked for half an hour. He never took his sunglasses off. It didn't seem like he had anywhere to be. And I didn't want to go home.

He told me he sat down with Earl Sweatshirt every few months so Earl could explain youth culture to him. He called him "Tebbe."

I told him about Camilla.

We smoked some. He told me he used to think Tony Hawk was corny, but then found out that Tony Hawk did worthwhile humanitarian work. Then he liked Tony Hawk. I asked him if we could take a picture together and he said, "Sure."

I gave my camera to a woman walking past us on the street and she took a picture.

He told me he felt old and had nostalgia for a time before the internet, and that he used a MetroPCS phone that didn't have internet. I told him I didn't remember a time before the internet.

I hoped he wouldn't get up and leave. He was warmer than I expected. The face of Supreme, my evil empire, tricking me into making a fool out of myself, being a poseur, a curse on the money my grandma left me when she died, cooler than I could ever be, an actuarial student from Woodmere who couldn't skateboard and didn't understand art, and too old… He was warm to me. Solicitous, even. He asked me questions.

I told him I couldn't skateboard. He laughed. He said, "That's cool."

And then he said he had to leave. He shook my hand again.

I said, "Thank you for talking to me. I feel like I haven't talked to anyone in a long time."

I spent three days sitting outside the Supreme store in London. I bought one thing every morning so they wouldn't shoo me off my bench.

CHAPTER LVII

We flew home to New York. When we got there, it was nighttime. It was snowing.

In the taxi on the way home from the airport, I looked through my pictures until I felt carsick. When we got to Camilla's house, we both got out.

She said, "Why are you getting out?"

I said, "Can I sleep on your couch? I don't want to go home."

She let me sleep on the couch.

She said good night and went into her room. I poked around in the kitchen for a while, looking for something to eat. I hadn't eaten since the airport in London, 20 hours before. But there were only ingredients.

I sat on the couch and looked for food on Seamless. All of the nearby restaurants were closed. And if I ordered from a restaurant that was like a mile away, the delivery guy would have to bike all that way in the snow. And then I would have had to give him a humane tip, at least $6 or $7.

I decided to go to sleep. I took 2 milligrams of Ativan with vodka and then three Mellow Yellows to fall asleep. More than I did on the trip, but my tolerance was high.

I got up off the couch and walked over to the window. I opened it and smoked one out the window. I stood there, looking out at the streetlights on Atlantic Avenue. I watched the snow falling. It would have been a nice picture. Frigid air blew in through the window.

I smoked about half the cigarette and felt unsteady on my feet. I felt disoriented. I looked around. I couldn't remember what I was doing there.

I stumbled into Camilla's room. She used her laptop in bed.

I said, "I don't feel good."

Camilla said, "That's a shame."

I said, "No, I really don't feel good."

Camilla said, "Why don't you lie down?"

I lurched towards her bed.

She said, "No, not in here! On the couch!"

I lay down on her bed.

I said, "I feel disoriented. I can't, like, I don't know. I can't."

CHAPTER LVIII

I woke up in the ambulance. They'd stuck me with an IV. Camilla sat on the seat in the back of the ambulance, crying. My jacket was next to her. I felt fucked up.

The IV in my arm reminded me of *The Simpsons* episode where Homer and Bart are spraying Interferon in Marge's hospital room and Dr. Hibbert says, "Good lord! You're wasting thousands of dollars of Interferon!" And then Homer says, "And you're 'interferon' with our good time!"

Camilla stopped crying when I opened my eyes and looked at her. She started crying again.

I said, "It's okay, I'm okay."

Camilla said, between sobs, "You're such a fucking idiot, I can't even fucking believe it."

I said, "But aren't you glad I waited until we got back to New York for this to happen though?"

Camilla didn't say anything. She sat there, shaking her head and running her hand through her hair. She was wearing sweat pants.

I said, "I've never seen you in sweat pants."

She said, "Can you promise you won't ever do this again?"

I said, "I didn't *mean* to do it. I didn't really have control over it. I didn't know this would happen. I only took the stuff I normally take and this has never happened before. I guess, maybe, I didn't know my limit. But now I know."

Camilla didn't say anything.

I said, "Did you tell my parents?"

Camilla didn't say anything.

I sat up and said, "No, seriously, did you tell them?"

Camilla shook her head.

I said, "Are you sure the ambulance was necessary? I think I could have slept it off."

Camilla said, "You weren't moving."

I said, "Did you shake me? To try to wake me up?"

Camilla said, "I carried you down the stairs."

I said, "But did you *shake* me? Or did you carry me gently?"

Camilla said, "I hate you."

I said, "I'm sorry."

Camilla closed her eyes and put her headphones on.

I turned to the paramedic, a black woman in her 30s. I asked, "Are they going to pump my stomach?"

The paramedic said, "The hospital staff makes that decision."

I said, "I know, but, like, in your medical opinion, do you think they will pump my stomach?"

The paramedic said, "Probably not."

I said, "Are you sure? Could you give me, like, ballpark? Ballpark percentage likelihood that they will?"

The paramedic smiled and shook her head. She liked me.

A minute passed.

I said, "Is this covered by my insurance?"

The paramedic said, "It depends on your insurance."

I said, "I have insurance through school. I think it's Aetna. Would that cover it?"

The paramedic said, "I really don't know."

Another minute passed.

I said, "Could you just drop me off at home? We're pretty close to my apartment."

CHAPTER LIX

They took me out of the ambulance and gave me a hospital gown. I stayed in a recovery room at the hospital in Fort Greene overnight. They gave me another IV. They didn't need to pump my stomach.

I watched my heartbeat on the monitor. Looked pretty healthy to me. I asked one of the nurses if it would be covered by my school insurance. She also said she didn't know.

Camilla slept in the chair in the hospital room overnight with her beanie pulled down over her eyes. I couldn't fall asleep. I looked at her skin under the unforgiving hospital fluorescent lights. Still looked good. I wished we could sleep together again, or I could at least climb out of bed and kiss her on the forehead, but I didn't want to unplug the IV.

I fell asleep and had a dream. In the dream, I went into the Supreme store on Lafayette Street. The employees saw me and dragged me out onto the sidewalk by the arms, one on each arm, like orderlies hauling an uncooperative patient in a mental institution.

I tried to kick them and screamed at them to just let me buy something. I threatened them: "If you don't let me, I'll just get it on eBay!" They beat me with skateboards but it didn't hurt. And then they tossed me into the street, heaving me by my arms and legs. A cab came towards me, closer and closer to running me over. I woke up.

CHAPTER LX

In the morning, the nurses made me fill out some forms. A doctor talked to me for a while and made me sign up for counseling. A nurse gave me some brochures and other literature about drug treatment.

I sat with Camilla in the waiting room while the hospital processed my insurance and other paperwork. I ate six or seven bags of chips and cookies from the vending machine and washed it down with a Diet Pepsi. Not quite a meal, but more than a snack.

I showed her the Supreme website on my phone. The 2015 season was out. She liked the fire extinguisher.

She said, "I don't think the fire extinguisher has an illicit connotation. Pretty much the opposite, actually."

I said, "You could hit someone on the head with it. Or extinguish the fire you start when you drop your marijuana on the carpet."

She laughed. I laughed too. I think I was joking.

I said, "You don't really hate me, do you?"

Camilla said, "I did when I said it, but I don't anymore."

I said, "I don't think you can only hate someone momentarily. That's not hate. Hate is between, like, cats and dogs. The Montagues and the Capulets. It's a state of affairs, not just a feeling."

Camilla shrugged.

She said, "What do you think of the season?"

I said, "It's awesome, like all the other ones."

She said, "Are you being serious?"

I said, "Of course. It's awesome. Everything they do is awesome in its way. Even the ugly stuff."

Outside the hospital, we stood on the street. We shared one. I tried not to slobber on it.

I said, "Thanks for bringing my jacket."

It was snowing and there were slush puddles all around us.

Camilla said, "That's it?"

I said, "Thanks for saving my life."

Camilla says, "I only did it so you would owe me."

I said, "But it would have been such a hassle for you if you hadn't. You would have had to be interviewed by the police and stuff. My parents would have sued you for negligence."

Camilla rolled her eyes. She said, "Should we get a cab?"

I said, "I feel like walking. I haven't exercised since we walked in Japan. And I have to get my bag from your apartment."

We started walking towards her apartment.

I put an appointment in my calendar to remind me to book another appointment with the psychiatrist who prescribed me the Ativan and Mellow Yellow and Propranalol. If he were to find out about the hospital visit, like if they put an alert out on me to not prescribe me anything anymore, I could have just said a finicky friend mistook my deep slumber for a fatal overdose.

We walked a few blocks. Camilla said, "Are you sure you can do it? You're walking slowly."

I said, "Yeah, it's like twenty minutes."

Camilla said, "I know, but, like…"

I said, "Really, I can handle it."

Camilla said, "Do you feel weak?"

I said, "I feel okay. Not different from a bad hangover. And I have 300 bad hangovers a year. We just have to walk slowly."

We walked down DeKalb Avenue towards Brooklyn Heights.

When we hit Flatbush Avenue Extension, I said, "Can we go to Supreme? It's just over the bridge."

Camilla said, "I thought you weren't allowed in."

I said, "Maybe I am and I don't know it."

CHAPTER LXI

We walked over the Manhattan Bridge. Through Chinatown, through Little Italy, to SoHo. I ate some more snacks
from a deli on the way. We both saw the Supreme sign at the
same time.

We walked towards Supreme and saw the line outside the
store. There was always a line after a new season came out. It
wasn't that long, only about a quarter of a block, because it
was snowing. Some people were deterred by the snow, but not
I.

She got on the line and I stood next to her. I leaned on her.
We waited for ten minutes and it didn't move. I fumbled with
the hospital band.

I said, "What are you thinking about?"

She said, "I don't know, nothing."

I said, "Tell me."

She half-smiled. She said, "Boners."

I said, "Why?"

She said, "They're so mysterious."

I said, "Why?"

She said, "I don't know. I just love them."

I fumbled with the hospital band again.

I said, "Do you think a hospital band is a cool accessory?"

She said, "No."

I said, "What if I wear it with –"

She said, "No. Just, no. Don't joke about it."

The line moved and we got closer. I pulled my hood over my head. I took my glasses off and put them in my pocket because they would make me more recognizable to the employee who'd kicked me out the last time.

I said, "Can I tell you another thing about the Talmud?"

Camilla said, "Please don't."

I said, "It's short."

She said, "Fine."

I said, "You can't intertwine cotton and wool. Like, to make a garment. They can't mix. I think really strict observers don't even wear cotton and wool at the same time, just to be safe."

Camilla said, "Why?"

I said, "I have no idea."

She said, "Why didn't you say *that* Talmud fact at dinner instead of the rape one?"

I said, "I don't know the rationale for not mixing cotton and wool. It's like telling the setup to a joke but without the punchline. In mixed company, you want me to tell half a joke? I don't think so."

CHAPTER LXII

Some people came out of the store and they let more in. They only let a few people into the store at a time because Supreme's only anti-theft mechanisms are the vigilance and menace of the employees. They needed to keep their eyes on the customers.

Then we were ten people away, then six, then three. We were next. I felt so nervous that they were going to kick me out. I was breathing fast. I tucked the hospital band under the sleeve of my jacket.

I said, "Are you sure you want to do this? We don't have to."

Camilla said, "Why wouldn't I? Are you sure *you* want to do this? You look pale."

I said, "I'm fine."

They let us in. I walked in, through the door, into Supreme New York. The lights were bright inside, brighter than in the other stores. I thought. Maybe they weren't.

I bought Camilla the fire extinguisher. She'd earned it. For myself, I bought t-shirt that said "You're not living… UNTIL YOUR LIVING FOR SUPREME!" with a picture of Jesus next to the text.

And two pill organizers that said s u p r e m e instead of m t w t f s s.

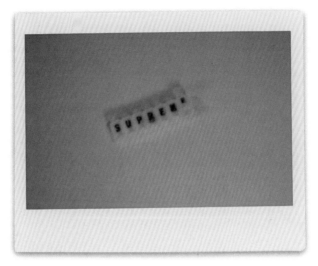

And a little knife.

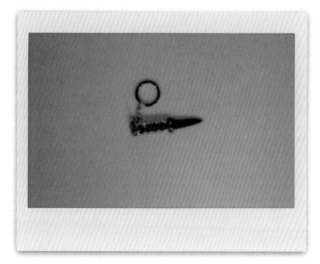

And a long-sleeve t-shirt with moth on it, the same moths as the *Silence of the Lambs* poster, the moth that covers Clarice's mouth.

The moths had a little hidden message inside them. A Satanic orgy. Salvador Dali. I didn't get it.

When I got up to the counter, the guy behind the counter was the same one who escorted me out the last time I was in the store. He looked at me and his eyes narrowed. He recognized me.

But he didn't stop me from buying my things. He didn't say anything to me, but he also didn't put any stickers into my bag. They would always put stickers into my bag before my story came out. Even when I bought stuff online, they put stickers into the box they shipped the stuff in.

We took an UberT back to Camilla's apartment. She got into bed. I ordered Thai food on Seamless for us for lunch. I took my jacket and shoes off. In the bathroom, I took my Flower Pants out of my suitcase and put them on.

I crawled into bed and curled up next to her, facing her, with my knees touching her thigh and my forehead touching her shoulder, with my arms pressed to my chest.

I had class at 8:30 a.m. the next day. I felt like a drink. I thought I would be able to convince Camilla to sleep with me at least one more time. She kissed me on the forehead and pet me, pet my hair, like a little dog. I loved how it felt. She kissed me again on the forehead. I would remember it. We waited for the food.